Joyce Carol Oates

ON BOXING

ecco
An Imprint of HarperCollins*Publishers*

Printed in the United States of America. No part of this book may be used or reproduced in any manner whatsoever without written permission except in the case of brief quotations embodied in critical articles and reviews. For information address HarperCollins Publishers Inc., 10 East 53rd Street, New York, NY 10022.

HarperCollins books may be purchased for educational, business, or sales promotional use. For information please write: Special Markets Department, HarperCollins Publishers Inc., 10 East 53rd Street, New York, NY 10022.

First Ecco edition published in 2002.

"On Boxing" originally published in 1987 as *On Boxing* by Dolphin/Doubleday.
"On Mike Tyson" originally published in 1988 in *(Woman) Writer: Occasions & Opportunities* by E. P. Dutton and Company. "The Cruelest Sport" originally appeared in *The New York Review of Books,* February 13, 1992.

Portions of "On Boxing" have appeared in earlier versions in *The New York Times* magazine, June 16, 1985 and *The Ontario Review,* Fall/Winter 1986.

Library of Congress Cataloging-in-Publication Data
Oates, Joyce Carol, 1938-
    On boxing / Joyce Carol Oates ; with photographs by John Ranard.
        p.   cm.
    Originally published: Garden City, N.Y. : Dolphin/Doubleday, 1987.
    1. Boxing.   I. Title.
GV1133.02   1994
    796.8′3—dc20   94-17428
        ISBN 0-88001-385-0
Cover photograph by John Ranard. Copyright © 1987 by John Ranard

    04 05 06 RRD 10 9 8 7 6 5 4

For the contenders . . .

CONTENTS

FOREWORD

No other subject is, for the writer, so intensely personal as boxing. To write about boxing is to write about oneself—however elliptically, and unintentionally. And to write about boxing is to be forced to contemplate not only boxing, but the perimeters of civilization—what it is, or should be, to be "human."

When I was writing *On Boxing*, in the grip of a curious, inexplicable compulsion, from February 1985 (when I drafted a short story titled "Golden Gloves"—I never understood why) to spring 1987, it happened that I was riding the crest, without knowing it, of a triumphant era in this turbulent and always precarious American "sport." The great, inimitable Muhammad Ali had retired, but Larry Holmes was an estimable, intrepid heavyweight champion. Marvin Hagler was a brilliant middleweight champion. The ingenious Sugar Ray Leonard, recently retired, was due soon to return—with unexpectedly spectacular results. There was Michael Spinks, there was Thomas Hearns, there was the buttery-smooth and seemingly invincible Donald Curry. There was, seemingly forever, Roberto Durán. There was the beloved Irish featherweight champion Barry McGuigan. And a Cus D'Amato-trained young man named Mike Tyson, whose first professional fight was in March 1985, was rapidly ascending the ranks of the heavyweight division by knock-outs. Like the legendary Harry Greb, Tyson seemed to be training by fighting, every two or three weeks, indefatigably. Tyson's career was so meteoric, and so self-consuming, that it has seemed as much moral exemplum as sports history: beginning in public glory, ending in public shame. (If, in fact, Tyson's career, after his conviction on charges of rape in February 1992, has ended.)

Much has changed in boxing since that time, though it has been hardly a decade. Virtually all of the reigning boxers have disappeared. The enormous purses of the 1980's—the theme of an entire chapter of *On Boxing*— have been multiplied tenfold for heavyweight title fights. The sport seems in crisis, its best practitioners no less than its most dubious contaminated by association with fixed fights, manipulated judges, questionable referees. Demands for its abolition are made, indignation is aroused, well-argued editorials are printed, deals continue to be made, boxers continue to be "managed." Occasionally there is a boxing match that, in its demonstration of skill, courage, intelligence, hope, seems to redeem the sport—or almost. Perhaps boxing has always been in crisis, a sport *of* crisis.

Without doubt, it is our most dramatically "masculine" sport, and our most dramatically "self-destructive" sport. In this, for some of us, its abiding interest lies.

JANUARY 1994

ON BOXING

It's a terrible sport, but it's a sport . . .
the fight for survival is the fight.
—ROCKY GRAZIANO,
former middleweight champion of the world

They are young welterweight boxers so evenly matched they might be twins, though one has a redhead's pallor and the other is a dusky-skinned Hispanic. Circling each other in the ring, beneath the glaring lights, trying jabs, tentative left hooks, right crosses that dissolve in mid-air or turn into harmless slaps. How to get inside! How to press an advantage, score a point or two, land a single punch! It seems they have forgotten all they've been trained to do and the Madison Square Garden fight crowd is getting noisy, derisive, impatient. Time is running out. "Those two—what'd they do, wake up this morning and decide they were boxers?" a man behind me says in disgust. (He's dark, nattily dressed, neat-trimmed moustache and tinted glasses. A sophisticated fight fan. Knows all the answers. Two hours later he will be screaming, "Tommy! Tommy! Tommy!" over and over in a paroxysm of grief as, on the giant closed-circuit television screen lowered over the ring, middleweight champion Marvelous Marvin Hagler batters his brash challenger Thomas Hearns into insensibility.)

The young welterweights are surely conscious of the chorus of jeers, boos, and catcalls in this great cavernous space reaching up into the cheap twenty-dollar seats in the balconies amid the constant milling of people in the aisles, the commingled smells of hotdogs, beer, cigarette and cigar smoke, hair oil. But they are locked desperately together in their futile match—circling, "dancing," jabbing, slapping, clinching—now a flurry of light blows, clumsy footwork, yet another sweaty stumbling despairing clinch into the ropes that provokes a fresh wave of derision as the referee helps them apart. Why are they here in the Garden of all places, each fighting, it seems, his first professional fight? Neither wants to hurt the other—neither is angry at the other. When the bell sounds at the end of the fourth and final round the crowd boos a little louder. The Hispanic boy, silky yellow shorts, damp frizzy floating hair, strides about his corner of the ring with his gloved hand aloft—not in defiance of the boos which increase in response to his gesture, or even in acknowledgment of them. It's just something he's doing, something he has seen older boxers do, he's saying *I'm here, I made it, I did it.*

When the decision is announced as a draw the crowd's derision increases in volume. "Get out of the ring!" "Assholes!" "Go home!" Contemptuous male laughter follows the boys up the aisle in their robes, towels about their heads, sweating, breathless. Why had *they* thought they were boxers?

· 2 ·

How can you enjoy so brutal a sport, people sometimes ask me.

Or pointedly don't ask.

And it's too complex to answer. In any case I don't "enjoy" boxing in the usual sense of the word, and never have; boxing isn't invariably "brutal"; and I don't think of it as a "sport."

Nor can I think of boxing in writerly terms as a metaphor for something else. No one whose interest began as mine did in childhood—as an offshoot of my father's interest—is likely to think of boxing as a symbol of something beyond itself, as if its uniqueness were merely an abbreviation, or iconographic; though I can entertain the proposition that life is a metaphor for boxing—for one of those bouts that go on and on, round following round, jabs, missed punches, clinches, nothing determined, again the bell and again and you and your opponent so evenly matched it's impossible not to see that your opponent *is* you: and why this struggle on an elevated platform enclosed by ropes as in a pen beneath hot crude pitiless lights in the presence of an impatient crowd?—that sort of hellish-writerly metaphor. Life *is* like boxing in many unsettling respects. But boxing is only like boxing.

For if you have seen five hundred boxing matches you have seen five hundred boxing matches and their common denominator, which certainly exists, is not of primary interest to you. "If the Host is only a symbol," as the Catholic writer Flannery O'Connor once remarked, "I'd say the hell with it."

I am a fighter who walks, talks, and thinks fighting, but I try not to look like it.
—MARVELOUS MARVIN HAGLER,
middleweight champion of the world

L ike a dancer, a boxer "is" his body, and is totally identified with it. And the body is identified with a certain weight:

HEAVYWEIGHT—no weight limit
CRUISERWEIGHT—not over 195 pounds
LIGHT HEAVYWEIGHT—not over 175 pounds
MIDDLEWEIGHT—not over 160 pounds
JUNIOR MIDDLEWEIGHT—not over 154 pounds
WELTERWEIGHT—not over 147 pounds
JUNIOR WELTERWEIGHT—not over 140 pounds
LIGHTWEIGHT—not over 135 pounds
JUNIOR LIGHTWEIGHT—not over 130 pounds
FEATHERWEIGHT—not over 126 pounds
JUNIOR FEATHERWEIGHT—not over 122 pounds

BANTAMWEIGHT—not over 118 pounds
FLYWEIGHT—not over 112 pounds

Though the old truism "A good big man will always beat a good little man" has been disproved any number of times (most recently by Michael Spinks in his victory over Larry Holmes) it is usually the case that a boxer invites disaster by fighting out of his weight division: he can "move up" but very likely he can't "bring his punch with him." Where at one time the distinctions between weight were fairly crude (paralleling life's unfairness—the mismatches of most battles outside the ring) boxing promoters and commissions have created a truly Byzantine hierarchy of weights to regulate present-day fights. In theory, the finely calibrated divisions were created to prevent mismatches; in practice, they have the felicitous effect of creating many more "champions" and many more lucrative "title" shots. So it is, an ambitious boxer in our time hopes not only to be a champion but to be a great champion—an immortal; he may try for multiple titles, like Sugar Ray Robinson (world welter- and middleweight champion who tried, and failed, to win the light-heavyweight title from Joey Maxim), Sugar Ray Leonard (world welter- and junior-middleweight champion), Roberto Durán (world light-, welter- and light-middleweight champion who tried, and failed, to move up to middleweight), Alexis Arguello (world featherweight, junior lightweight, and lightweight champion who hoped for a junior welterweight title before his recent retirement).

In order to make his weight the boxer may resort to fasting or vigorous exercise so close to fight time that he risks serious injury: like, most recently, WBA bantamweight champion Richie Sandoval who lost ten pounds in a short period of time and, in his match with Gaby Canizales in March 1986, nearly lost his life as a consequence. When Michael Spinks made boxing history in September 1985 by becoming the first light-heavyweight to win the heavyweight title, as much excited media attention was paid to Spinks's body as to his boxing. For Spinks had accomplished what constituted a *tour de force* of the physical—with the help of his trainer and nutritionist he had created for himself a true heavyweight's body: two hundred pounds of solid muscle. And though his opponent Larry Holmes outweighed him by twenty-odd pounds it scarcely mattered since Spinks had not merely gained weight, he had become a "new" body. And he sustained this remarkable new body for his title defense against Holmes, which he also won. Boxing's fanaticism can go no further.

*Why are you a boxer, Irish featherweight
champion Barry McGuigan was asked. He said:
"I can't be a poet. I can't tell stories . . ."*

Each boxing match is a story—a unique and highly condensed drama without words. Even when nothing sensational happens: then the drama is "merely" psychological. Boxers are there to establish an absolute experience, a public accounting of the outermost limits of their beings; they will know, as few of us can know of ourselves, what physical and psychic power they possess—of how much, or how little, they are capable. To enter the ring near-naked and to risk one's life is to make of one's audience voyeurs of a kind: boxing is so intimate. It is to ease out of sanity's consciousness and into another, difficult to name. It is to risk, and sometimes to realize, the agony of which *agon* (Greek, "contest") is the root.

In the boxing ring there are two principal players, overseen by a shadowy third. The ceremonial ringing of the bell is a summoning to full wakefulness for both boxers and spectators. It sets into motion, too, the authority of Time.

The boxers will bring to the fight everything that is themselves, and everything will be exposed—including secrets about themselves they cannot fully realize. The physical self, the maleness, one might say, underlying the "self." There are boxers possessed of such remarkable intuition, such uncanny prescience, one would think they were somehow recalling their fights, not fighting them as we watch. There are boxers who perform skillfully, but mechanically, who cannot improvise in response to another's alteration of strategy; there are boxers performing at the peak of their talent who come to realize, mid-fight, that it will not be enough; there are boxers—including great champions—whose careers end abruptly, and irrevocably, as we watch. There has been at least one boxer possessed of an extraordinary and disquieting awareness not only of his opponent's every move and anticipated move but of the audience's keenest shifts in mood as well, for which he seems to have felt personally responsible— Cassius Clay / Muhammad Ali, of course. "The Sweet Science of Bruising" celebrates the physicality of men even as it dramatizes the limitations, sometimes tragic, more often poignant, of the physical. Though male spectators identify with boxers no boxer behaves like a "normal" man when he is in the ring and no combination of blows is "natural." All is style.

Every talent must unfold itself in fighting. So Nietzsche speaks of the Hellenic past, the history of the "contest"—athletic, and otherwise—by which Greek youths were educated into Greek citizenry. Without the ferocity of competition, without, even, "envy, jealousy, and ambition" in the contest, the Hellenic city, like the Hellenic man, degenerated. If death is a risk, death is also the prize—for the winning athlete.

In the boxing ring, even in our greatly humanized times, death is always a possibility—which is why some of us prefer to watch films or tapes of fights already past, already defined as history. Or, in some instances, art. (Though to prepare for writing this mosaic-like essay I saw tapes of two infamous "death" fights of recent times: the Lupe Pintor–Johnny Owen bantamweight match of 1982, and the Ray Mancini–Duk Koo-Kim lightweight match of the same year. In both instances the boxers died as a consequence of their astonishing resilience and apparent indefatigability—their "heart," as it's known in boxing circles.) Most of the time, however, death in the ring is extremely unlikely; a statistically rare possibility like your possible death tomorrow morning in an automobile accident or in next month's headlined airline disaster or in a freak accident involving a fall on the stairs or in the bathtub, a skull fracture, subarachnoid hemorrhage. Spectators at "death" fights often claim afterward that what happened simply seemed to happen—unpredictably, in a sense accidentally. Only in retrospect does death appear to have been inevitable.

If a boxing match is a story it is an always wayward story, one in which anything can happen. And in a matter of seconds. Split seconds! (Muhammad Ali boasted that he could throw a punch faster than the eye could follow, and he may have been right.) In no other sport can so much take place in so brief a period of time, and so irrevocably.

Because a boxing match is a story without words, this doesn't mean that it has no text or no language, that it is somehow "brute," "primitive," "inarticulate," only that the text is improvised in action; the language a dialogue between the boxers of the most refined sort (one might say, as much neurological as psychological: a dialogue of split-second reflexes) in a joint response to the mysterious will of the audience which is always that the fight be a worthy one so that the crude paraphernalia of the setting —ring, lights, ropes, stained canvas, the staring onlookers themselves—be erased, forgotten. (As in the theater or the church, settings are erased by way, ideally, of transcendent action.) Ringside announcers give to the wordless spectacle a narrative unity, yet boxing as performance is more clearly akin to dance or music than narrative.

To turn from an ordinary preliminary match to a "Fight of the Century" like those between Joe Louis and Billy Conn, Joe Frazier and Muhammad Ali, Marvin Hagler and Thomas Hearns is to turn from listening or half-listening to a guitar being idly plucked to hearing Bach's *Well-Tempered Clavier* perfectly executed, and that too is part of the story's mystery: so much happens so swiftly and with such heart-stopping subtlety you cannot absorb it except to know that something profound is happening and it is happening in a place beyond words.

I try to catch my opponent on the tip of his nose
because I try to punch the bone into his brain.
—*MIKE TYSON,*

Boxing's claim is that it is superior to life in that it is, ideally, superior to all accident. It contains nothing that is not fully willed.

The boxer meets an opponent who is a dream-distortion of himself in the sense that his weaknesses, his capacity to fail and to be seriously hurt, his intellectual miscalculations—all can be interpreted as strengths belonging to the Other; the parameters of his private being are nothing less than boundless assertions of the Other's self. This is dream, or nightmare: my strengths are not fully my own, but my opponent's weaknesses; my failure is not fully my own, but my opponent's triumph. He is my shadow-self, not my (mere) shadow. The boxing match as "serious, complete, and of a certain magnitude"—to refer to Aristotle's definition of tragedy—is an event that necessarily subsumes both boxers, as any ceremony subsumes its participants. (Which is why one can say, for instance, that the greatest fight of Muhammad Ali's career was one of the few fights Ali lost—the first heroic match with Frazier.)

The old boxing adage—a truism surely untrue—that you cannot be knocked out if you see the blow coming, and if you *will* yourself not to be knocked out, has its subtler, more daunting significance: nothing that happens to the boxer in the ring, including death—"his" death—is not of his own will or failure of will. The suggestion is of a world-model in which we are humanly responsible not only for our own acts but for those performed against us.

Which is why, though springing from life, boxing is not a metaphor for life but a unique, closed, self-referential world, obliquely akin to those severe religions in which the individual is both "free" and "determined"— in one sense possessed of a will tantamount to God's, in another totally helpless. The Puritan sensibility would have understood a mouth filling with blood, an eye popped out of its socket—fit punishment for an instant's negligence.

A boxing trainer's most difficult task is said to be to persuade a young boxer to get up and continue fighting after he has been knocked down. And if the boxer has been knocked down by a blow he hadn't seen coming— which is usually the case—how can he hope to protect himself from being knocked down again? and again? The invisible blow is after all—invisible.

"Normal" behavior in the ring would be unbearable to watch, deeply shameful: for "normal" beings share with all living creatures the instinct to persevere, as Spi-

noza said, in their own being. The boxer must somehow learn, by what effort of will non-boxers surely cannot guess, to inhibit his own instinct for survival; he must learn to exert his "will" over his merely human and animal impulses, not only to flee pain but to flee the unknown. In psychic terms this sounds like magic. Levitation. Sanity turned inside out, "madness" revealed as a higher and more pragmatic form of sanity.

The fighters in the ring are time-bound—surely nothing is so excruciatingly long as a fiercely contested three-minute round—but the fight itself is timeless. In a sense it becomes all fights, as the boxers are all boxers. By way of films, tapes, and photographs it quickly becomes history for us, even, at times, art. Time, like the possibility of death, is the invisible adversary of which the boxers—and the referee, the seconds, the spectators—are keenly aware. When a boxer is "knocked out" it does not mean, as it's commonly thought, that he has been knocked unconscious, or even incapacitated; it means rather more poetically that he has been knocked out of Time. (The referee's dramatic count of ten constitutes a metaphysical parenthesis of a kind through which the fallen boxer must penetrate if he hopes to continue in Time.) There are in a sense two dimensions of Time abruptly operant: while the standing boxer is *in time* the fallen boxer is *out of time.* Counted out, he is counted "dead"—in symbolic mimicry of the sport's ancient tradition in which he would very likely be dead. (Though, as we may recall, the canny Romans reserved for themselves as spectators the death blow itself: the triumphant gladiator was obliged to wait for a directive from outside the arena before he finished off his opponent.)

If boxing is a sport it is the most tragic of all sports because more than any human activity it consumes the very excellence it displays—its drama is this very consumption. To expend oneself in fighting the greatest fight of one's life is to begin by necessity the downward turn that next time may be a plunge, an abrupt fall into the abyss. *I am the greatest* says Muhammad Ali. *I am the greatest* says Marvelous Marvin Hagler. You always think you're going to win, Jack Dempsey wryly observed in his old age, otherwise you couldn't fight at all. The punishment—to the body, the brain, the spirit—a man must endure to become even a moderately good boxer is inconceivable to most of us whose idea of personal risk is largely ego-related or emotional. But the punishment as it begins to show in even a young and vigorous boxer is closely gauged by his rivals, who are waiting for him to slip. (After junior-welterweight champion Aaron Pryor won a lackluster fight last year a younger boxer in his weight division, interviewed at ringside, said with a smile: "My mouth is watering." And there was twenty-nine-year-old Billy Costello's bold statement—"If I can't beat an old man [of thirty-three] then I should retire"—shortly before his bout with Alexis Arguello, in which he was knocked out in an early round.)

In the ring, boxers inhabit a curious sort of "slow" time—amateurs never box beyond three rounds, and for most amateurs those nine minutes are exhausting—while outside the ring they inhabit an alarmingly accelerated time. A twenty-three-year-old boxer is no longer young in the sense in which a twenty-three-year-old man is young; a thirty-five-year-old is frankly old. (Which is why Muhammad Ali made a tragic mistake in continuing his career after he had lost his title for the second time—to come out of retirement, aged thirty-eight, to fight Larry Holmes; and why Holmes made a similar mistake, years later, in needlessly exposing himself to injury, as well as professional embarrassment, by meeting with the light-heavyweight champion Michael Spinks. The victory of the thirty-seven-year-old Jersey Joe Walcott over the thirty-year-old Ezzard Charles, for the heavyweight title in 1951, is *sui generis*. And Archie Moore is *sui generis*.) All athletes age rapidly but none so rapidly and so visibly as the boxer.

So it is, the experience of watching great fighters of the past is radically different from having seen them perform when they were reigning champions. Jack Johnson, Jack Dempsey, Joe Louis, Sugar Ray Robinson, Rocky Marciano, Muhammad Ali, Joe Frazier—as spectators we know not only how a fight but how a career ends. The trajectory not merely of ten or fifteen rounds but that of an entire life . . .

> *Everything that man esteems*
> *Endures a moment or a day.*
> *Love's pleasure drives his love away,*

The painter's brush consumes his dreams;
The herald's cry, the soldier's tread
Exhaust his glory and his might:
Whatever flames upon the night
Man's own resinous heart has fed.

—WILLIAM BUTLER YEATS, *from "The Resurrection"*

When I see blood, I become a bull.
—MARVIN HAGLER

I have no difficulty justifying boxing as a sport because I have never thought of it as a sport.

There is nothing fundamentally playful about it; nothing that seems to belong to daylight, to pleasure. At its moments of greatest intensity it seems to contain so complete and so powerful an image of life—life's beauty, vulnerability, despair, incalculable and often self-destructive courage—that boxing *is* life, and hardly a mere game. During a superior boxing match (Ali-Frazier I, for instance) we are deeply moved by the body's communion with itself by way of another's intransigent flesh. The body's dialogue with its shadow-self—or Death. Baseball,

· 18 ·

football, basketball—these quintessentially American pastimes are recognizably sports because they involve play: they are games. One *plays* football, one doesn't *play* boxing.

Observing team sports, teams of adult men, one sees how men are children in the most felicitous sense of the word. But boxing in its elemental ferocity cannot be assimilated into childhood. (Though very young men box, even professionally, and many world champions began boxing in their early or mid-teens. By the time he was sixteen Jack Dempsey, rootless and adrift in the West, was fighting for small sums of money in unrefereed saloon fights in which—in the natural course of things—he might have been killed.) Spectators at public games derive much of their pleasure from reliving the communal emotions of childhood but spectators at boxing matches relive the murderous infancy of the race. Hence the occasional savagery of boxing crowds—the crowd, largely Hispanic, that cheered as the Welshman Johnny Owen was pounded into insensibility by the Mexican bantamweight champion Lupe Pintor, for instance—and the excitement when a man begins to seriously bleed.

Marvelous Marvin Hagler, speaking of blood, is speaking, of course, of his own.

Considered in the abstract the boxing ring is an altar of sorts, one of those legendary spaces where the laws of a nation are suspended: inside the ropes, during an officially regulated three-minute round, a man may be killed at his opponent's hands but he cannot be legally murdered. Box-

ing inhabits a sacred space predating civilization; or, to use D. H. Lawrence's phrase, before God was love. If it suggests a savage ceremony or a rite of atonement it also suggests the futility of such gestures. For what possible atonement is the fight waged if it must shortly be waged again . . . and again? The boxing match is the very image, the more terrifying for being so stylized, of mankind's collective aggression; its ongoing historical madness.

I hate to say it, but it's true—
I only like it better when pain comes.
—FRANK "THE ANIMAL" FLETCHER,
former middleweight contender

Years ago in the early 1950s when my father first took me to a Golden Gloves boxing tournament in Buffalo, New York, I asked him why the boys wanted to fight one another, why they were willing to get hurt. As if it were an explanation my father said, "Boxers don't feel pain quite the way we do."

Pain, in the proper context, is something other than pain.

Consider: Gene Tunney's single defeat in a thirteen-year career of great distinction was to a notorious fighter named Harry Greb who seems to have been, judging from boxing lore, the dirtiest fighter in history. Greb was infamous for his fouls—low blows, butting, "holding and hitting," rubbing his laces against an opponent's eyes, routine thumbing—as well as for a frenzied boxing style in which blows were thrown from all directions. (Hence, "The Human Windmill.") Greb, who died young, was a world middleweight champion for three years but a flamboyant presence in boxing circles for a long time. After the first of his several fights with Greb the twenty-two-year-old Tunney was so badly hurt he had to spend a week in bed; he'd lost an astonishing two quarts of blood during the fifteen-round fight. Yet, as Tunney said some years later:

> *Greb gave me a terrible whipping. He broke my nose, maybe with a butt. He cut my eyes and ears, perhaps with his laces . . . My jaw was swollen from the right temple down the cheek, along under the chin and partway up the other side. The referee, the ring itself, was full of blood . . . But it was in that first fight, in which I lost my American light-heavyweight title, that I knew I had found a way to beat Harry eventually. I was fortunate, really. If boxing in those days had been afflicted with the Commission doctors we have today—*

*who are always poking their noses into the ring and
examining superficial wounds—the first fight with Greb
would have been stopped before I learned how to beat
him. It's possible, even probable, that if this had happened I would never have been heard of again.*

Tunney's career, in other words, was built upon pain.
Without it he would never have moved up into Dempsey's
class.

Tommy Loughran, light-heavyweight champion in
the years 1927–29, was a master boxer greatly admired
by other boxers. He approached boxing literally as a science—as Tunney did—studying his opponents' styles and
mapping out ring strategy for each fight, as boxers and
their trainers commonly do today. Loughran rigged up
mirrors in his basement so that he could watch himself as
he worked out, for, as he said, no boxer ever sees himself
quite as he appears to his opponent. He sees the opponent
but not himself as an opponent. The secret of Loughran's
career was that his right hand broke easily so that he was
forced to use it only once each fight: for the knockout
punch or nothing. "I'd get one shot then the agony of the
thing would hurt me if the guy got up," Loughran said.
"Anybody I ever hit with a left hook I knocked flat on his
face, but I would never take a chance for fear if my [left
hand] goes, I'm done for."

Both Tunney and Loughran, it is instructive to note,
retired from boxing well before they were forced to retire.
Tunney became a highly successful businessman, and

Loughran a highly successful sugar broker on the Wall
Street commodities market. (Just to suggest that boxers
are not invariably stupid, illiterate, or punch-drunk.)

Then there was Carmen Basilio!—much loved for his
audacious ring style, his hit-and-be-hit approach. Basilio
was world middle- and welterweight champion 1953–57,
stoic, determined, a slugger willing to get hit in order to
deal powerful counter-punches of his own. Onlookers mar-
veled at the punishment Basilio seemed to absorb though
Basilio insisted that he didn't get hit the way people believed. And when he was hit, and hit hard—

> *People don't realize how you're affected by a knockout
> punch when you're hit on the chin. It's nerves is all it
> is. There's no real concussion as far as the brain is
> concerned. I got hit on the point of the chin [in a match
> with Tony DeMarco in 1955]. It was a left hook that
> hit the right point of my chin. What happens is it pulls
> your jawbone out of your socket from the right side and
> jams it into the left side and the nerve there paralyzed
> the whole left side of my body, especially my legs. My
> left knee buckled and I almost went down, but when I
> got back to my corner the bottom of my foot felt like it
> had needles about six inches high and I just kept stamp-
> ing my foot on the floor, trying to bring it back. And by
> the time the bell rang it was all right.*

Basilio belongs to the rough-and-tumble era of LaMotta,
Graziano, Zale, Pep, Saddler; Gene Fullmer, Dick Tiger,
Kid Gavilan. An era when, if two boxers wanted to fight

dirty, the referee was likely to give them license, or at least not to interfere.

Of Muhammad Ali in his prime Norman Mailer observed, "He worked apparently on the premise that there was something obscene about being hit." But in fights in his later career, as with George Foreman in Zaire, even Muhammad Ali was willing to be hit, and to be hurt, in order to wear down an opponent. Brawling fighters—those with "heart" like Jake LaMotta, Rocky Graziano, Ray Mancini—have little choice but to absorb terrible punishment in exchange for some advantage (which does not in any case always come). And surely it is true that some boxers (see Jake LaMotta's autobiographical *Raging Bull*) invite injury as a means of assuaging guilt, in a Dostoyevskian exchange of physical well-being for peace of mind. Boxing is about being hit rather more than it is about hitting, just as it is about feeling pain, if not devastating psychological paralysis, more than it is about winning. One sees clearly from the "tragic" careers of any number of boxers that the boxer prefers physical pain in the ring to the absence of pain that is ideally the condition of ordinary life. If one cannot hit, one can yet be hit, and know that one is still alive.

It might be said that boxing is primarily about maintaining a body capable of entering combat against other well-conditioned bodies. Not the public spectacle, the fight itself, but the rigorous training period leading up to it demands the most discipline, and is believed to be the chief cause of the boxer's physical and mental infirmities. (As a boxer ages his sparring partners get younger, the game itself gets more desperate.)

The artist senses some kinship, however oblique and one-sided, with the professional boxer in this matter of training. This fanatic subordination of the self in terms of a wished-for destiny. One might compare the time-bound public spectacle of the boxing match (which could be as brief as an ignominious forty-five seconds—the record for a title fight!) with the publication of a writer's book. That which is "public" is but the final stage in a protracted, arduous, grueling, and frequently despairing period of preparation. Indeed, one of the reasons for the habitual attraction of serious writers to boxing (from Swift, Pope, Johnson to Hazlitt, Lord Byron, Hemingway, and our own Norman Mailer, George Plimpton, Ted Hoagland, Wilfrid Sheed, Daniel Halpern, et al.) is the sport's systematic cultivation of pain in the interests of a project, a life-goal: the willed transposing of the sensation we know as pain (physical, psychological, emotional) into its polar opposite. If this is masochism—and I doubt that it is, or that it is simply—it is also intelligence, cunning, strategy. It is an act of consummate self-determination—the constant re-establishment of the parameters of one's being. To not only accept but to actively invite what most sane creatures avoid—pain, humiliation, loss, chaos—is to experience the present moment as already, in a sense, past. *Here* and *now* are but part of the design of *there* and *then:* pain now

but control, and therefore triumph, later. And pain itself is miraculously transposed by dint of its context. Indeed, it might be said that "context" is all.

The novelist George Garrett, an amateur boxer of some decades ago, reminisces about his training period:

> I learned something . . . about the brotherhood of boxers. People went into this brutal and often self-destructive activity for a rich variety of motivations, most of them bitterly antisocial and verging on the psychotic. Most of the fighters I knew of were wounded people who felt a deep, powerful urge to wound others at real risk to themselves. In the beginning. What happened was that in almost every case, there was so much self-discipline required and craft involved, so much else besides one's original motivations to concentrate on, that these motivations became at least cloudy and vague and were often forgotten, lost completely. Many good and experienced fighters (as has often been noted) become gentle and kind people . . . They have the habit of leaving all their fight in the ring. And even there, in the ring, it is dangerous to invoke too much anger. It can be a stimulant, but is very expensive of energy. It is impractical to get mad most of the time.

Of all boxers it seems to have been Rocky Marciano (still our only undefeated heavyweight champion) who trained with the most monastic devotion; his training methods have become legendary. In contrast to reckless fighters like Harry "The Human Windmill" Greb, who kept in condition by boxing all the time, Marciano was willing to seclude himself from the world, including his wife and family, for as long as three months before a fight. Apart from the grueling physical ordeal of this period and the obsessive preoccupation with diet and weight and muscle tone, Marciano concentrated on one thing: the upcoming fight. Every minute of his life was defined in terms of the opening second of the fight. In his training camp the opponent's name was never mentioned in Marciano's hearing, nor was boxing as a subject discussed. In the final month Marciano would not write a letter since a letter related to the outside world. During the last ten days before a fight he would see no mail, take no telephone calls, meet no new acquaintances. During the week before the fight he would not shake hands. Or go for a ride in a car, however brief. No new foods! No dreaming of the morning after the fight! For all that was not *the fight* had to be excluded from consciousness. When Marciano worked out with a punching bag he saw his opponent before him, when he jogged he saw his opponent close beside him, no doubt when he slept he "saw" his opponent constantly— as the cloistered monk or nun chooses by an act of fanatical will to "see" only God.

Madness?—or merely discipline?—this absolute subordination of the self. In any case, for Marciano, it worked.

Tommy Hearns was a little cocky, and I had something for him.
—MARVIN HAGLER

No sport is more physical, more direct, than boxing. No sport appears more powerfully homoerotic: the confrontation in the ring—the disrobing—the sweaty heated combat that is part dance, courtship, coupling—the frequent urgent pursuit by one boxer of the other in the fight's natural and violent movement toward the "knockout": surely boxing derives much of its appeal from this mimicry of a species of erotic love in which one man overcomes the other in an exhibition of superior strength and will. The heralded celibacy of the fighter-in-training is very much a part of boxing lore: instead of focusing his energies and fantasies upon a woman the boxer focuses them upon an opponent. Where Woman has been, Opponent must be.

As Ali's Bundini Brown has said: "You got to get the hard-on, and then you got to keep it. You want to be careful not to lose the hard-on, and cautious not to come."

Most fights, however fought, end with an embrace

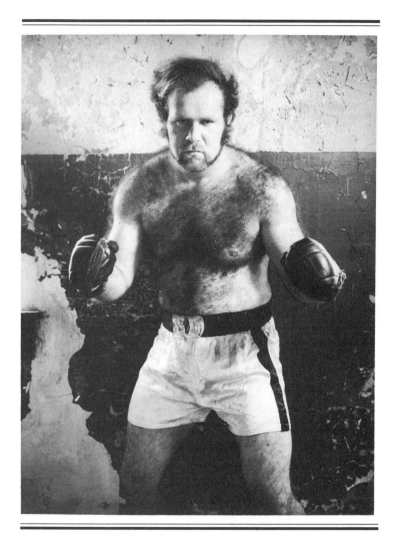

between the boxers after the final bell—a gesture of mutual respect and apparent affection that appears to the onlooker to be more than perfunctory. Rocky Graziano sometimes kissed his opponents out of gratitude for the fight. One might wonder if the boxing match leads irresistibly to this moment: the public embrace of two men who otherwise, in public or in private, could never approach each other with such passion. Though many men are loudly contemptuous of weakness (as if eager to dissociate themselves from it: as during a boxing match when one or both boxers are unwilling to fight) a woman is struck by the admiration, amounting at times to awe, they will express for a man who has exhibited superior courage while losing his fight. And they will express tenderness for injured boxers, even if it is only by way of commentary on photographs: the picture of Ray Mancini after his second defeat by Livingstone Bramble, for instance, when Mancini's face was hideously battered (photographs in *Sports Illustrated* and elsewhere were gory, near-pornographic); the much-reprinted photograph of the defeated Thomas Hearns being carried to his corner in the arms of an enormous black man (a bodyguard, one assumes) in solemn formal attire—Hearns the "Hit Man" now helpless, semiconscious, looking very like a black Christ taken from the cross. These are powerful, haunting, unsettling images, cruelly beautiful, inextricably bound up with boxing's primordial appeal.

Yet to suggest that men might love and respect one another directly, without the violent ritual of combat, is to misread man's greatest passion—for war, not peace. Love, if there is to be love, comes second.

I know I'm not a bad fighter. I try so hard at something I like doing. I love boxing. I dream of being a fighter. I see myself winning the title. I don't know which one. I see myself being picked up, carried around, getting my belt. Sometimes I see it in slow motion . . .
                    —a thirty-four-year-old welterweight
                         who has lost nearly all his fights,
                                    usually by knockouts

An "opponent" is known in the boxing trade as a man who loses, and is dependable. Matched with a younger, promising boxer with financial backing he will give a decent showing, he will very likely not collapse in the opening seconds of the opening round, and he will not, certainly, mar the record of the other boxer. He may have dreams of winning a "title" but his value to the trade is that he helps to build up (i.e., to inflate) another boxer's record. His name is always unknown—indeed, he is likely to have several names or aliases. His career is a foregone conclusion: he has none. He works for a living by way of being a human punching bag.

Opponents are also known as "stiffs" and "bums"— as in Joe Louis's "Bum-of-the-Month" matches after Louis had cleared the heavyweight division of serious contenders for his title.

The world's consistently highest-paid athletes are American boxers but it does not follow that boxers as a class are the highest paid athletes. The very opposite is the case. Impoverished people prostitute themselves in ways available to them, and boxing on its lowest levels offers an opportunity for men to make a living of a kind. In fact, if a boxer is fortunate and isn't injured, boxing will pay him better wages than most of the jobs available to unskilled and uneducated men in our post-industrial society. (After Michael Spinks won an Olympic gold medal he quit boxing and went to work scrubbing floors and cleaning toilets in a St. Louis chemical factory. But conditions in the factory were so bad he had to return, he said, to boxing: "Heck, breathing those chemicals, I could have died faster there than in the ring.") And boxing in circumstances where casino gambling and not safety is a priority—Atlantic City, for instance, and not New York City with its stringent boxing regulations—is likely to be highly tempting. The top of the pyramid is small, the base broad, shading out into the anonymous subsoil of humanity.

The Ring magazine, "The Bible of Boxing," publishes the results of over one thousand fights in every issue. Even boxing's many ranked and overrated boxers constitute a small number of the men who are licensed to box in the United States and elsewhere. *The Ring Record Book* lists such boxers as Johnny D. (who has lost sixteen fights in a row, twelve by knockouts); Marcus D. (who won only his first fight years ago and has lost each subsequent match); Obie G. (who has had nine fights and has been knocked out nine times); Irving B. (who has had seven fights and has been knocked out seven times, always in the first or second round). It is such professional opponents who account for the unblemished records of others —for clearly, the up-and-coming with their straight wins and zero losses cannot have been fighting one another.

(During the 1920s when boxing was officially banned in New York, boxers fought in private clubs, not unlike speakeasies, in wholly unsupervised circumstances. Budd Schulberg writes that during the years boxing was outlawed there were in fact many more matches in New York City than there are now: each borough had its own clubs, matches were held every night of the week, boxers of all weights, ages, experience, and abilities were thrown haphazardly together, and, if a match resulted in death, the boxer's body was likely to be dumped without identification in the river.)

With the complicity of managers and promoters, boxers of this class frequently fight under several aliases, and even with present-day regulations (in New York and Pennsylvania, for instance, a fighter who has been knocked out is automatically suspended for ninety days; in New Jersey, for sixty days) it is extremely difficult to prevent them from doing themselves harm. Desperation for money or simply for "fame" cannot be regulated. Identification is made not with boxing's limitless supply of losers but with boxing's very few stars, as in any other profession in which the individual can be, by way of his own intransigent will, glorified. As a trainer of opponents says, perhaps not even cynically: "There's a new guy walking in the gym every day."

When you're fighting you're fighting
for one thing: money.
—JACK DEMPSEY,
former heavyweight champion of the world

T hat boxing is our most controversial sport, always, it seems, on the very threshold of oblivion, has not prevented it from having become a multimillion-dollar business.

For the past several years the three highest-paid athletes in the world have been American boxers. (In 1985 Larry Holmes reported an income of a little more than

$6.5 million; Marvin Hagler, a little more than $5 million; Thomas Hearns, approximately $5 million. By contrast, the fourth highest-paid athlete, a celebrated football player, reported an income of only—only!—$3 million.) In his long and spotty career Jack Dempsey earned $3,500,000—prodigious for his time, though the equivalent today of only $28 million. Muhammad Ali, who earned somewhere beyond $70 million through his long career, is generally believed to be the most highly paid athlete in world history; his successor Larry Holmes is believed to have earned nearly that much. (Though figures vary, and Holmes's career, at the time of this writing, is still extant; he claims to have $99 million in the bank— with more to come.) Individual boxing matches sometimes bring in extraordinary sums for boxers, even accounting for the money drawn off by promoters: the losing challenger Thomas Hearns made at least $7 million in his eight-minute fight with Marvin Hagler, while Hagler made at least $7.5 million; for the first of his highly publicized matches with Roberto Durán in 1980—which he lost on points—the popular welterweight champion Sugar Ray Leonard was paid $10 million (to Durán's $2 million). One of the focal arguments for a title fight between Marvin Hagler and Sugar Ray Leonard was that the gate would very likely be the highest in all of boxing history: a promoter's dream. And none of these figures takes into account various subsidiary earnings from television appearances and commercials which, in Leonard's case, have certainly been substantial.

Indeed, these subsidiary earnings have become, for many boxers, the measure of their worth beyond the ring: the assessment, in dollars, of "consumer acceptance" of their images. *(The Ring* magazine is beginning to note the sums earned by boxers giving television endorsements of products . . . a new kind of ring "record," it might be said.)

Money has drawn any number of retired boxers back into the ring, frequently with tragic results. The most notorious example still remains Joe Louis, who, in a desperate attempt to pay money owed in back taxes, continued fighting well beyond the point at which he could defend himself against younger heavyweights. After a career of seventeen years during which Louis virtually came to typify boxing internationally he was finally—and ignominiously—stopped by the much younger Rocky Marciano (who was as grieved by his victory as Louis by the defeat). Louis then took on a degrading second career as a professional wrestler, which ended abruptly in 1956 when, aged forty-two, he suffered injuries to his heart muscles after three-hundred-pound "Rocky Lee" stepped on his chest.

Ezzard Charles, Jersey Joe Walcott, Joe Frazier, Muhammad Ali, most recently Larry Holmes—each heavyweight champion or ex-champion continued fighting well beyond the point at which he could safely defend himself. If Ali had retired permanently at the age of thirty-six—if he had not, contrary to his physician's advice, insisted upon fighting, two years later, the much-younger Larry Holmes—perhaps his story would have a happier ending. (When Ali was told in the mid-1970s to retire by his personal physician Ferdie Pacheco his response was to fire Pacheco.) Of all heavyweight champions only Rocky Marciano, to whom fame and money were evidently not of paramount importance, was wise enough to retire before he was defeated.

In any case, a boxer's passion for money—for the prodigious sums earned by a very few champions—does not account for the fact that a public is willing, if not eager, to pay them these sums. Private and public obsessions mimic one another but are not identical.

> *Boxing is the sport to which*
> *all other sports aspire.*
> *—GEORGE FOREMAN,*
> former heavyweight champion of the world

At least in theory and by way of tradition boxing is a sport. But what *is* sport?—and why is a man, *in* sport, not the man he is or is expected to be at other times?

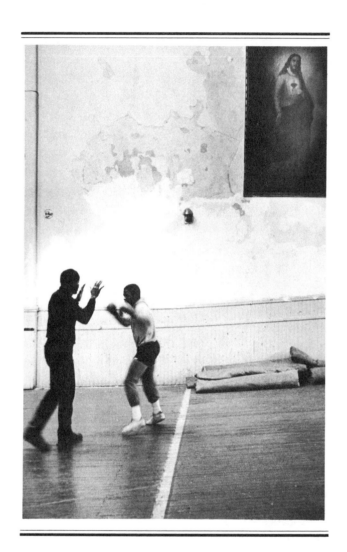

Consider the history of gladiatorial combat as the Romans practiced it, or caused it to be practiced, from approximately 265 B.C. to its abolishment by Theodoric in A.D. 500. In the ancient world, among part-civilized nations, it was customary after a battle to sacrifice prisoners of war in honor of commanders who had been killed. It also became customary to sacrifice slaves at the funerals of all persons of importance. But then—for what reason?—for amusement, or for the sake of "sport"?—the condemned slaves were given arms and urged to defend themselves by killing the men who were ordered to kill them. Out of this evolution of brute sacrifice into something approaching a recognizable sporting contest the notorious phenomenon of Roman gladitorial combat—death as mass amusement—gradually arose. Surely there is nothing quite like it in world history.

At first the contests were performed at the funeral pyre or near the sepulcher, but, with the passage of time, as interest in the fighting detached itself from its ostensibly religious context, matches were moved to the Forum, then to the Circus and amphitheaters. Contractors emerged to train the slaves, men of rank and political importance began to keep "families" of gladiators, upcoming fights were promoted and advertised as sporting contests are today, shows lasting as long as three days increased in number and popularity. Not the mere sacrifice of helpless individuals but the "sport" of the contest excited spectators, for, though the instinct to fight and to kill is surely qualified by one's personal courage, the instinct to watch others fight and kill is evidently inborn. When the boxing fan shouts, "Kill him! Kill him!" he is betraying no peculiar individual pathology or quirk but asserting his common humanity and his kinship, however distant, with the thousands upon thousands of spectators who crowded into the Roman amphitheaters to see gladiators fight to the death. That such contests for mass amusement endured not for a few years or even decades but for centuries should arrest our attention.

According to Petronius the gladiators took the following oath: "We swear, after the dictation of Eumolpus, to suffer death by fire, bonds, stripes, and the sword; and whatever else Eumolpus may command, as true gladiators we bind ourselves body and mind to our master's service." Their courage became legendary. Cicero referred to it as a model for all Roman citizens—that one should be willing to suffer nobly in the defense of the Commonwealth. In general, gladiators were slaves and condemned criminals who could hope to prolong their lives or even, if they were champions, to gain freedom; but impoverished freemen often fought as well. With the passage of time, paralleling and surely contributing to what we see as the decadence of Rome, even men of rank volunteered to compete publicly. (Under Nero, that most notorious of Roman emperors, such wild exhibitions flourished. It is estimated that during his reign from A.D. 54 to 68 as many as one thousand aristocrats performed as gladiators in one way or another, in fights fair, handicapped, or fixed. At times even women of rank competed—which matches were no doubt particularly noteworthy.) So drawn to these violent sports were Roman aristocrats that the Emperor Augustus was finally moved to issue an edict forbidding them to train as gladiators.

The origins of gladiatorial boxing are specifically Greek. According to tradition a ruler named Thesus (circa 900 B.C.) was entertained by the spectacle of two matched fighters, seated, facing each other, hammering each other to death with their fists. Eventually the men fought on their feet and covered their fists with leather thongs; then with leather thongs covered with sharp metal spikes—the cestus. A ring of some kind, probably a circle, became a neutral space to which an injured boxer might temporarily retreat. When the Romans cultivated the sport it became extremely popular: one legendary cestus-champion was said to have killed 1,425 opponents. Winning gladiators were widely celebrated as "kings of athletes" and heroes for all. By confirming in the public arena the bloody mortality of other men they established for themselves, as champions always do, a kind of immortality.

So it happens that the wealthier and more advanced a society, the more fanatic its interest in certain kinds of sport. Civilization's trajectory is to curve back upon itself —naturally? helplessly?—like the mythical snake biting its own tail and to take up with passion the outward signs and gestures of "savagery." While it is plausible that emotionally effete men and women may require ever more extreme experiences to arouse them, it is perhaps the case too that the desire is not merely to *mimic* but, magically, to *be* brute, primitive, instinctive, and therefore innocent. One might then be a person for whom the contest is not mere self-destructive play but life itself; and the world, not in spectacular and irrevocable decline, but new, fresh, vital, terrifying and exhilarating by turns, a place of wonders. It is the lost ancestral self that is sought, however futilely. Like those dream-remnants of childhood that year by year continue to elude us but are never abandoned, still less despised, for that reason.

Roman gladiatorial combat was abolished under the Christian emperors Constantine and Theodoric, and its practice discontinued forever. Boxing as we know it in the United States derives solely from English bare-knuckle prizefighting of the eighteenth century and from an entirely different conception of sport.

The first recorded account of a bare-knuckle fight in England—between "a gentleman's footman and a butcher"—is dated 1681 and appeared in a publication called the *London Protestant Mercury*. This species of fight, in which maiming and death were not the point, was known as a "Prize Fight" or the "Prize Ring," and was public entertainment of an itinerant nature, frequently attached to village fairs. The Prize Ring was a movable space created by spectators who formed a loose circle by holding a length of rope; the Prize Fight was a voluntary contest between two men, usually a "champion" and a "challenger," unrefereed but governed by rudimentary rules of fair play. The challenge to fight was put to a

crowd by a fighter and his accomplices and if any man
wanted to accept he tossed his hat into the ring—hence
the political expression with its overtone of bellicosity—
and the fight was on. Bets were commonly placed on
which man would knock the other down first or draw
"first blood." Foul play was actively discouraged by the
crowd; the fighters shook hands after the fight. "The Noble Art," as prizefighting was called, began as a low-life
species of entertainment but was in time enthusiastically
supported by sporting members of the aristocracy and the
upper classes.

England's earliest bare-knuckle champion was a man
named James Figg who won the honor in 1719. The last
of the bare-knuckle champions was the American heavyweight John L. Sullivan whose career—from approximately 1882 to 1892—overlapped both bare-knuckle
fighting and gloved boxing as established under the rules
of the Marquis of Queensberry which are observed, with
some elaboration, to the present time. The most significant changes were two: the introduction of leather gloves
(mainly to protect the hand, not the face—a man's knuck-
les are easily broken) and the third man in the ring, the
referee, whose privilege it is to stop the fight at his own
discretion, if he thinks a boxer has no chance of winning
or cannot defend himself against his opponent. With the
introduction of the referee the crudeness of "The Noble
Art" passes over into the relative sophistication of boxing.

The "third man in the ring," usually anonymous so far as the crowd is concerned, appears to many observers no more than an observer himself, even an intruder; a ghostly presence as fluid in motion and quick-footed as the boxers themselves (indeed, he is frequently an ex-boxer). But so central to the drama of boxing is the referee that the spectacle of two men fighting each other unsupervised in an elevated ring would seem hellish, if not obscene—life rather than art. The referee makes boxing possible.

The referee is our intermediary in the fight. He is our moral conscience extracted from us as spectators so that, for the duration of the fight, "conscience" need not be a factor in our experience; nor need it be a factor in the boxers' behavior. (Asked if boxers are ever sorry for having hurt their opponents, Carmen Basilio replied: "Sorry? Are you kidding? Boxers are never sorry.") Which is not to say that boxers are always and forever without conscience: all boxers are different, and behave differently at different times. But there are occasions when a boxer who is trapped in the ropes and unable to fall to the canvas while being struck repeatedly is in danger of being killed unless the referee intervenes—the attacking boxer has been trained not to stop his attack while his opponent is still technically standing. In the rapidly escalating intensity of the fight only the referee remains neutral and objective.

Though the referee's role is highly demanding and it has been estimated that there are perhaps no more than a dozen really skilled referees in the world, it seems necessary in the drama of the fight that the referee himself possesses no dramatic identity: referees' names are rarely remembered after a fight except by seasoned boxing fans. Yet, paradoxically, the referee's participation is crucial. He cannot control what happens in the ring but he can control to a degree *that* it happens—he is responsible for the fight if not for the individual fighters' performances. In a match in which boxing skills and not merely fighting are predominant the referee's role can be merely functional, but in a fiercely contested match it is of incalculable importance. The referee holds the power of life and death at certain times since his decision to terminate a fight, or to allow it to continue, can determine a boxer's fate. (One should know that a well-aimed punch with a heavyweight's full weight behind it can have the equivalent force of ten thousand pounds—a blow that must be absorbed by the brain in its jelly sac.) In the infamous Benny Paret–Emile Griffith fight of March 1962 the referee Ruby Goldstein was said to have stood paralyzed as Griffith trapped Paret in the ropes, striking him as many as eighteen times in the head. (Paret died ten days later.) Boxers are trained not to quit. If knocked down, they try to get up to continue the fight, even if they can hardly defend themselves. The primary rule of the ring—to defend oneself at all times—is both a parody and a distillation of life.

In the past—well into the 1950s—it was not customary for a referee to interfere with a fight, however brutal and one-sided. A boxer who kept struggling to his feet after having been knocked down, or, like the intransigent Jake LaMotta in his sixth and final fight with Sugar Ray Robinson in 1951, refused to fall to the canvas though he could no longer defend himself and had become a human punching bag, was simply left to his fate. The will of the crowd—and overwhelmingly it *is* the will of the crowd— that one man defeat the other totally and irrevocably, was honored. Hence the bloody "great" fights of boxing's history—Dempsey's triumph over Willard, for instance—inconceivable today.

It should be understood that "boxing" and "fighting," though always combined in the greatest of boxers, can be entirely different and even unrelated activities. Amateur boxers are trained to win their matches on points; professionals usually try for knockouts. (Not that professionals are more violent than amateurs but why trust judges?—and the knockout is dramatically spectacular.) If boxing is frequently, in the lighter weights especially, a highly complex and refined skill, belonging solely to civilization, fighting belongs to something predating civilization, the instinct not merely to defend oneself—for how has the masculine ego ever been assuaged by so minimal a response to threat?—but to attack another and to force him into absolute submission. This accounts for the electrifying effect upon a typical fight crowd when fighting suddenly emerges out of boxing—when, for instance, a boxer's face begins to bleed and the fight seems to enter a new and more dangerous phase. The flash of red is the visible sign of the fight's authenticity in the eyes of many spectators and boxers are justified in being proud, as many are, of their facial scars.

If the "violence" of boxing seems at times to flow from the crowd, to be a heightened expression of the crowd's delirium—rarely transmitted by television, by the way—the many restraints and subtleties of boxing are possible because of the "third man in the ring," a counter of sorts to the inchoate wash of emotion beyond the ropes and the ring apron: our conscience, as I've indicated, extracted from us, and granted an absolute authority.

> *. . . Whether [this] makes me a humanist*
> *or a voyeur, I'm not sure.*
> *—JOHN SCHULIAN,*
> sportswriter

Writers have long been attracted to boxing, from the early days of the English Prize Ring to the present time. Its most immediate appeal is that of the spectacle, in itself wordless, lacking a language, that requires others to define it, celebrate it, complete it. Like all extreme but perishable human actions boxing excites not

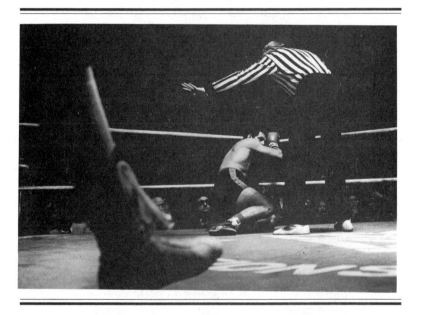

only the writer's imagination, but also his instinct to bear witness. Before film and tape, this instinct must have been particularly acute. (Consider a sport that often took place illegally, many of its most famous fights fought on barges, on islands, in outlaw territory between states, involving the risk of arrest for both performers and observers: what passion!) And boxers have frequently displayed themselves, inside the ring and out, as characters in the literary sense of the word. *Extravagant fictions without a structure to contain them.*

In the days of the Prize Ring, accounts of fights were often in verse, accompanied by cartoon-like drawings, printed on broadsides, and sold by itinerant salesmen. From approximately 1700 onward—according to boxing historian Pierce Egan—most English newspapers, including the fashionable *The Times,* carried detailed accounts of fights; and in 1818 Egan brought out the first edition of his famous *Boxiana: Sketches of Ancient and Modern Pugilism,* which covered the Prize Ring from its earliest days to Egan's own when, though wildly popular, Prize Fighting was officially illegal and announcements of impending matches were by way of rumor. (Any number of editions of *Boxiana* have been printed, the most recent being in the 1970s.) Egan's zest for his outlaw subject is communicated in prose of a particularly vigorous kind—colorful, direct, blunt, "masculine," yet as subtly and as wittily nuanced as that of his eighteenth-century predecessors Defoe, Swift, Pope, Fielding, Churchill. It is Egan who called fighting "the Sweet Science of Bruising" and it is

Egan whom A. J. Liebling most frequently cites and acknowledges as his master in *The Sweet Science,* a *boxiana* of modern times much admired by boxing enthusiasts.

(I sense myself uneasily alone in disliking much of Liebling, for his relentlessly jokey, condescending, and occasionally racist attitude toward his subject. Perhaps because it was originally published in *The New Yorker* in the early 1950s *The Sweet Science: Boxing and Boxiana—a Ringside View* is a peculiarly self-conscious assemblage of pieces, arch, broad in its humor, rather like situation comedy in which boxers are "characters" depicted for our amusement. Liebling is uncertain even about such champions as Louis, Marciano, and Robinson—should one revere, or mock? And he is pitiless when writing about "Hurricane" Jackson, a black boxer cruelly called an animal, an "it," because of his poor boxing skills and what Liebling considers his mental inferiority. The problem for Liebling and for *The New Yorker* must have been how to sell a blood sport like boxing to a genteel, affluent readership to whom the idea of men fighting for their lives would have been deeply offensive; how to suggest boxing's drama while skirting boxing's tragedy. It is a problem that, for all his verbal cleverness, Liebling never entirely solves.)

A good deal has been made of Ernest Hemingway's attraction to boxing yet Hemingway never wrote about boxing with the sympathy or perception with which he wrote about bullfighting; "Fifty Grand" and "The Battler" are not among Hemingway's best short stories, and

his portrait of the "Princeton middleweight" Robert Cohn
in *The Sun Also Rises* is a startlingly crude piece of Jew-
baiting, in which Cohn's boxing skills are irrelevant.
(When, provoked beyond endurance, Cohn knocks down
Jake Barnes and his drunken friend, the scene passes by
so swiftly it makes virtually no impression on the reader.)

Far more canny and knowledgeable is Norman
Mailer, whose essays on Cassius Clay/Muhammad Ali and
his coevals, and on the "aesthetics of the arena" generally, are as good as anything ever written on the subject.
Mailer's strength lies in his recognition that the boxers
are *other*—though he does not say so, even in the long
extravagant meditation of *The Fight* (its title in homage to
Hazlitt's great essay), it seems clear to this reader at least
that Mailer cannot establish a connection between himself
and the boxers: he tries heroically but he cannot understand them and so he is forever excluded from what, un-
thinkingly, they represent: an ideal (because unthinking,
unforced) masculinity, beyond all question. It is this recognition of his exclusion—an exclusion very nearly as
complete as, say, the exclusion of a woman from boxing's
codified world—that allows for the force of Mailer's vision. And since the great champions of our time have
been black, Mailer's preoccupation with masculinity is a
preoccupation with blackness as well. Hence these characteristic flights of metaphysical fancy that strike the ear
with the poignancy of a lovesick lament:

*If [the heavyweights] become champions they begin to
have inner lives like Hemingway or Dostoyevsky, Tol-
stoy or Faulkner, Joyce or Melville or Conrad or Lawrence or Proust . . . Dempsey was alone and Tunney
could never explain himself and Sharkey could never
believe himself nor Schmeling nor Braddock, and Carnera was sad and Baer an indecipherable clown; great
heavyweights like Louis had the loneliness of the ages
in their silence, and men like Marciano were mystified
by a power which seemed to have been granted them.
With the advent, however, of the great modern Black
heavyweights, Patterson, Liston, then Clay and Frazier,
perhaps the loneliness gave way to what it had been
protecting itself against—a surrealistic situation unsta-
ble beyond belief. Being a Black heavyweight champion in the second half of the twentieth century (with
Black revolutions opening all over the world) was now
not unlike being Jack Johnson, Malcolm X and Frank
Costello all in one . . .*

(EXISTENTIAL ERRANDS, *"King of the Hill"*)

It cannot be a coincidence that everyone's favorite boxing
novel, Leonard Gardner's *Fat City*, is a novel less about
boxing than about the strategies of self-deception; a hand-
book of sorts in failure, in which boxing functions as the
natural activity of men totally unequipped to comprehend
life. The boxers of Gardner's Stockton, California—that
notorious fight town—seem to exist in a world claustrophobic as a training gym, with no more awareness of the

great boxers of their time (would not Cassius Clay himself have been their contemporary?) than of politics and "society" in general. *Fat City* is the underside of the American dream, in which men with some minimal skill in a dangerous sport are hired to fight one another for pitifully small purses: it is a measure of the novel's irony that victory, for such stakes, is hardly to be distinguished from failure. Leonard Gardner seems to have written no other fiction, but his several articles on boxing—published in such magazines as *Sports Illustrated* and *Esquire*—display a remarkable gift for realizing, as if from the inside, the psychology of the man born to fight, the man who knows nothing *but* fighting, no matter the suicidal nature of his calling.

W. C. Heinz and Ted Hoagland have written highly regarded novels about boxing, *The Professional* and *The Circle Home* respectively, though Hoagland's novel is something of an anomaly: there are no fights in it, only training scenes, rendered with a mesmerizing kinetic precision. Budd Schulberg, Irwin Shaw, Nelson Algren, Ring Lardner, James Farrell, John O'Hara, Jack London—all have written stories about boxers, of varying worth and seriousness.

What might be called the romance of boxing—and even the sordid, filmed, *is* romance—underlies a number of Hollywood movies of similarly uneven worth, the most extraordinary being Martin Scorsese's award-winning *Raging Bull*, in which Robert De Niro almost literally transforms himself into Jake LaMotta. Other notable films

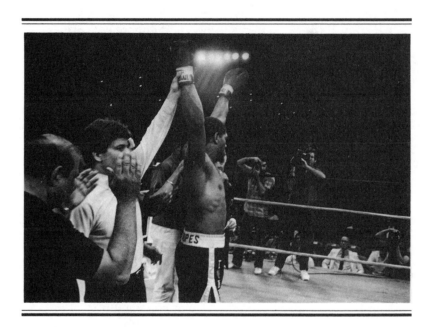

in this genre are *Fat City, Champion, Somebody Up There Likes Me* (based on the Rocky Graziano autobiography), *The Harder They Fall, The Set-Up, The Champ, Body and Soul, Requiem for a Heavyweight,* and *The Great White Hope*—the last two based on successful plays. And then there are the "Rocky" movies, scarcely about boxing as we know it (Rocky and his heavyweight opponents are, for one thing, ludicrously encumbered with bodybuilders' physiques, not boxers') but effective as pop-iconographic success stories starring Sylvester Stallone as Rocky, "The Italian Stallion," the sweet tough guy, the perpetual underdog who cannot lose even against overwhelming odds. Rocky is a comic book boxer, his matches are comic book matches, like the exploits of his look-alike Rambo, who embodies even more powerfully than Rocky America's fascination with the (male) *isolato* whose orientation to the world is purely physical. Yet it is significant, certainly, that Stallone made Rocky a boxer, in homage to heavyweight champion Rocky Marciano, whose ring style he imitates—to a degree.

Boxing has often stimulated first-rate sportswriting, that most taxing of genres. Among contemporary sportswriters John Schulian (of the Philadelphia *Daily News)* and Hugh McIlvanney (of the English *The Observer)* are outstanding for the consistently high quality of their prose and for what might be called their rigorously analytical approach to their subject: not merely *what,* and *how,* but in fact *why*—why does boxing exist, why are men (and some women) fascinated by it, what does it tell us about the human predicament? Schulian's *Writers' Fighters* and McIlvanney's *McIlvanney on Boxing* bring together columns published over a period of time but are notable for the unity of their respective visions. Neither writer takes his subject for granted, nor does he draw back from examining the ambivalent relationship between the man who writes about boxing and boxing itself, "the sweet science of bruising." Other sports draw forth other responses, but boxing is, here as elsewhere, a special case. In no other sport is the connection between performer and observer so intimate, so frequently painful, so unresolved.

That no other sport can elicit such *theoretical* anxiety lies at the heart of boxing's fascination for the writer. It is the thing in itself but it is also its meaning to the individual, shifting and problematic as a blurred image in a mirror. The writer contemplates his opposite in the boxer, who is all public display, all risk and, ideally, improvisation: he will know his limit in a way that the writer, like all artists, never quite knows his limit—for we who write live in a kaleidoscopic world of ever-shifting assessments and judgments, unable to determine whether it is revelation or supreme self-delusion that fuels our most crucial efforts. Setting aside for a moment the problem of incompetent or biased judges, of the kind that gave Michael Spinks a victory over Larry Holmes in Spinks's title defense of April 1986, or had Ray Mancini outpointing Livingstone Bramble in the first of their two matches, the boxer's world is not an ambiguous one: he quickly comes to know his worth in a context of other boxers. Indeed, it is impossible not to know it. "Promising" careers are ended in a matter of seconds; "comebacks" are revealed as mere mistakes; a young and unranked contender (like "Lightning" Lonnie Smith in his title match against junior welterweight champion Billy Costello) leaps immediately to the top. There can be no ambiguity about Marvin Hagler's defeat of John Mugabi, or Thomas Hearns's defeat of James Shuler, or the unexpected loss of his bantamweight title by Richie Sandoval to Gaby Canizales— the near loss, it seemed to some observers, of Sandoval's very life. This sense of an ending, a limit, a final and incontestable judgment—boxing in its greatest moments suggests the bloody fifth acts of classic tragedies, in which that mysterious element we call "plot" achieves closure.

For some writers the fascination has to do, as I've suggested earlier, with boxing's dazzlingly explicit display of masochism—"masochism" in its loosest, most suggestive, one might say poetic sense. For, contrary to stereotyped notions, boxing is primarily about being, and not giving, hurt. (Which the most distinguished boxing movies—*Raging Bull, Fat City, Champion*—suggest most graphically.) To move through pain to triumph—or the semblance of triumph—is the writer's, as it is the boxer's, hope. The moment of visceral horror in a typical fight, at least as I experience it, is that moment when one boxer loses control, cannot maintain his defense, begins to waver, falter, fall back, rock with his opponent's punches which he can no longer absorb; the moment in which the fight is turned around, and which an entire career, an entire life, may end. It is not an isolated moment but *the* moment—mystical, universal. The defeat of one man is the triumph of the other: but we are apt to read this "triumph" as merely temporary and provisional. Only the defeat is permanent.

When I used to dream about boxing, or about abstract, inconclusive matches between dream-opponents whose faces I could not see, I thought of boxing as a knot of sorts, tightly, cruelly knotted, there to be untied. You can't, but you must, untie it. You must—but you can't. If you untie one knot you will be confronted with another and beyond that another, and another: rounds, matches, career, "life." The difference for the boxer is that loss, humiliation, shame are only part of the risk—physical injury, even death, awaits as well. One is punished for one's failure as Kafka imagined one might be punished for one's sins, the sentence etched into flesh, killing even as it pronounces judgment.

. . . Down there in the stable a hollow square of faces in the lantern light, the white faces on three sides, the black faces on the fourth, and in the center two of [Sutpen's] wild negroes fighting, naked, fighting not as white men fight, with rules and weapons, but as negroes fight to hurt one another quick and bad.
    —from WILLIAM FAULKNER'S ABSALOM, ABSALOM!

Some time ago one of the southern states adopted a new method of capital punishment. Poison gas supplanted the gallows. In its earliest stages, a microphone was placed inside the sealed death chamber so that scientific observers might hear the words of the dying prisoner . . . The first victim was a young Negro. As the pellet dropped into the container, and gas curled upward, through the microphone came these words: "Save me, Joe Louis. Save me, Joe Louis. Save me, Joe Louis . . ."

—MARTIN LUTHER KING, JR.,
quoted in Chris Mead,
CHAMPION—JOE LOUIS,
BLACK MAN IN WHITE AMERICA

*It's hard being black. You ever been black?
I was black once—when I was poor.*
—LARRY HOLMES,
former WBC heavyweight champion

One's first impression is that professional boxers fighting together appear to be angry with each other, since their actions mimic anger, even rage. Why else hit, and try to injure, another person? Naturally this initial impression is misleading—boxing is "work" to most boxers and emotion has little part in it, or should have little. Indeed, highly successful champions from Jack Dempsey to Larry Holmes have insisted they fought only for money. To acknowledge other motives would suggest *machismo's* vulnerability.

Yet in a deeper sense boxers *are* angry, as even a superficial knowledge of their lives indicates. And boxing is fundamentally about anger. It is in fact the only sport in which anger is accommodated, ennobled. It is the only human activity in which rage can be transposed without equivocation into art.

Some observers—among them men—believe that boxers are angry because they are men; and anger, for men, is a means of asserting dominance over other men— a tool, one might say, of the manly trade. Yet it is reasonable to assume that boxers fight one another because the legitimate objects of their anger are not accessible to them. There is no political system in which the spectacle of two men fighting each other is not a striking, if unintended, image of the political impotence of most men (and women): You fight what's nearest, what's available, what's ready to fight you. And, if you can, you do it for money.

If boxers as a class are angry one would have to be willfully naïve not to know why. For the most part they constitute the disenfranchised of our affluent society, they are the sons of impoverished ghetto neighborhoods in which anger, if not fury, is appropriate—rather more, perhaps, than Christian meekness and self-abnegation. (It

was only in prison that Sonny Liston, one of twenty-five children born to a sharecropper's family in rural Arkansas, had enough to eat.) Where there is peace, Nietzsche theorizes, the warlike man attacks himself, but what precisely is "peace"? and where, in ghetto neighborhoods of unspeakable squalor and malaise, is it to be located? Boxing may be a way of cruelly assaulting one's self but it is most immediately a way of transcending one's fate. Going to war, like Marvin Hagler, and making millions of dollars from it, is distinctly American.

The history of boxing—of fighting—in America is very much one with the history of the black man in America. It hardly needs to be said that the armed services of recent times are comprised disproportionately of black youths; this was particularly evident in the Vietnam War. Perhaps it is less well known that in the American South, before the Civil War, white slave owners commonly pitted their Negro slaves against one another in combat, and made bets on the results. To prevent the slaves' escape, or, perhaps, to make poetically graphic the circumstances of the black men's degradation, iron collars resembling dog chains were fixed about their necks and attached to chains. Often the fights were to the death. The onlookers, of course, were white; and male.

"Fighting slave collars," as they are called, are sometimes exhibited as artifacts of a specifically American/Southern history; sometimes as instruments of torture.

At the present time, when most outstanding boxers

are black, Hispanic, or Mexican, purely "Caucasian" men begin to look anemic in the ring; a white-skinned champion (the enormously popular Barry McGuigan, for instance) is something of an anomaly, and white-skinned contenders (Gerry Cooney, Matthew Hilton, Gene Hatcher, et al.) very much in demand. One of the most popular athletes in Canada is the young welterweight Shawn O'Sullivan, so alarmingly *white* a figure in the ring, in the first fight of his televised for an American audience, the viewer sensed almost at once that his more experienced black opponent, Simon Brown, would handily defeat him. The anxieties of an earlier era—that black men would prove more "manly" than white men if allowed to fight them in fair, public fights—would seem to have come true.

It is perhaps not commonly known that a Negro heavyweight championship title existed from 1902 to 1932 when many white champions (including John L. Sullivan, Jim Jeffries, Jack Dempsey) refused to fight blacks. (In 1925 Dempsey pointedly refused to meet Harry Wills —"The Black Menace"—in a title fight urged upon him by many observers.) One wonders: who were the true world's champions in those years? And of what value are historical records when they record so blatantly the prejudices of a dominant race? As recently as 1982, after decades of exemplary black boxers—from Jack Johnson to Joe Louis to Sugar Ray Robinson to Muhammad Ali— heavyweight champion Larry Holmes drew racist slurs

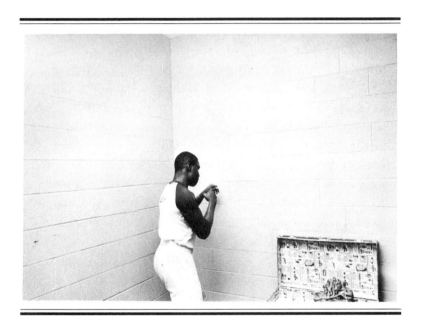

and insults when he defended his title against the overrated and overpromoted White Hope challenger Gerry
Cooney (whose prefight picture, and not Holmes's, ran on
the cover of *Time* magazine). It is said that on the day of
the match in Las Vegas President Reagan's Secret Service
installed a special telephone hookup in Cooney's dressing
room so that the white boxer could be immediately con-
gratulated if he won; there was no matching telephone in
the black champion's dressing room.

Much has been made of Holmes's legendary bitterness, as if having earned millions of dollars—and millions
of dollars for others—should tidily erase the humiliations
of the past. Surely this is a psychological impossibility?
Lashing out against the memory of Rocky Marciano after
the first of his two controversial losses to Michael Spinks,
Holmes may well have been lashing out against all white
champions: "—to be technical: Rocky Marciano couldn't
carry my jockstrap."

Men and women with no personal or class reason for
feeling anger are inclined to dismiss the emotion, if not
piously condemn it, in others. Why such discontent? why
such unrest? why so *strident?* Yet this world is conceived
in anger—and in hatred, and in hunger—no less than it is
conceived in love: that is one of the things that boxing is
about. It is so simple a thing it might be overlooked.

Those whose aggression is masked, or oblique, or
unsuccessful, will always condemn it in others. They are

likely to think of boxing as "primitive"—as if inhabiting the flesh were not a primitive proposition, radically inappropriate to a civilization supported by and always subordinate to physical strength: missiles, nuclear warheads. The terrible silence dramatized in the boxing ring is the silence of nature before man, before language, when the physical being alone was God.

In any case, anger is an appropriate response to certain intransigent facts of life, not a motiveless malignancy as in classic tragedy but a fully motivated and socially coherent impulse. Impotence takes many forms—one of them being the reckless physical expenditure of physical potency.

What time is it?—"Macho Time"!
—HECTOR *"MACHO MAN"* CAMACHO,
WBC lightweight champion

I don't want to knock my opponent out.
I want to hit him, step away, and watch him hurt.
I want his heart.
—*JOE FRAZIER*,
former heavyweight champion of the world

A fairy-tale proposition: the heavyweight champion is the most dangerous man on earth: the most feared, the most manly. His proper mate is very likely the fairy-tale princess whom the mirrors declare the fairest woman on earth.

Boxing is a purely masculine activity and it inhabits a purely masculine world. Which is not to suggest that most men are defined by it: clearly, most men are not. And though there are female boxers—a fact that seems to surprise, alarm, amuse—women's role in the sport has always been extremely marginal. (At the time of this writing the most famous American woman boxer is the black

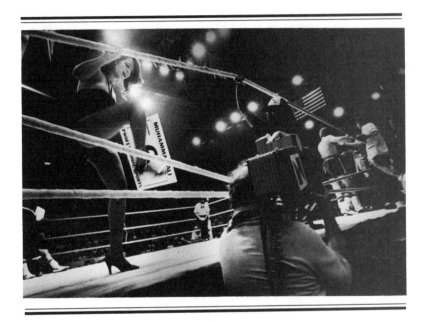

champion Lady Tyger Trimiar with her shaved head and theatrical tiger-striped attire.) At boxing matches women's role is limited to that of card girl and occasional National Anthem singer: stereotypical functions usually performed in stereotypically zestful feminine ways—for women have no natural place in the spectacle otherwise. The card girls in their bathing suits and spike heels, glamour girls of the 1950s, complement the boxers in their trunks and gym shoes but are not to be taken seriously: their public exhibition of themselves involves no risk and is purely decorative. Boxing is for men, and is about men, and *is* men. A celebration of the lost religion of masculinity all the more trenchant for its being lost.

In this world, strength of a certain kind—matched of course with intelligence and tirelessly developed skills—determines masculinity. Just as a boxer is his body, a man's masculinity is his use of his body. But it is also his triumph over another's use of his body. The Opponent is always male, the Opponent is the rival for one's own masculinity, most fully and combatively realized. Sugar Ray Leonard speaks of coming out of retirement to fight one man, Marvin Hagler: "I want Hagler. I need that man." Thomas Hearns, decisively beaten by Hagler, speaks of having been obsessed with him: "I want the rematch badly . . . there hasn't been a minute or an hour in any day that I haven't thought about it." Hence women's characteristic repugnance for boxing per se coupled with an intense interest in and curiosity about men's fascination with it. Men fighting men to determine worth (i.e., masculinity) excludes women as completely as the female experience of childbirth excludes men. And is there, perhaps, some connection?

In any case, raw aggression is thought to be the peculiar province of men, as nurturing is the peculiar province of women. (The female boxer violates this stereotype and cannot be taken seriously—she is parody, she is cartoon, she is monstrous. Had she an ideology, she is likely to be a feminist.) The psychologist Erik Erikson discovered that, while little girls playing with blocks generally create pleasant interior spaces and attractive entrances, little boys are inclined to pile up the blocks as high as they can and then watch them fall down: "the contemplation of ruins," Erikson observes, "is a masculine specialty." No matter the mesmerizing grace and beauty of a great boxing match, it is the catastrophic finale for which everyone waits, and hopes: the blocks piled as high as they can possibly be piled, then brought spectacularly down. Women, watching a boxing match, are likely to identify with the losing, or hurt, boxer; men are likely to identify with the winning boxer. There is a point at which male spectators are able to identify with the fight itself as, it might be said, a Platonic experience abstracted from its particulars; if they have favored one boxer over the other, and that boxer is losing, they can shift their loyalty to the winner—or, rather, "loyalty" shifts, apart from conscious volition. In that way the ritual of fighting is always honored. The high worth of combat is always affirmed.

Boxing's very vocabulary suggests a patriarchal

world taken over by adolescents. This world is young. Its focus is youth. Its focus is of course *macho—machismo* raised beyond parody. To enter the claustrophobic world of professional boxing even as a spectator is to enter what appears to be a distillation of the masculine world, empty now of women, its fantasies, hopes, and stratagems magnified as in a distorting mirror, or a dream.

Here, we find ourselves through the looking-glass. Values are reversed, evaginated: a boxer is valued not for his humanity but for being a "killer," a "mauler," a "hitman," an "animal," for being "savage," "merciless," "devastating," "ferocious," "vicious," "murderous." Opponents are not merely defeated as in a game but are "decked," "stiffed," "starched," "iced," "destroyed," "annihilated." Even the veteran sportswriters of so respectable a publication as *The Ring* are likely to be pitiless toward a boxer who has been beaten. Much of the appeal of Roberto Durán for intellectual boxing *aficionados* no less than for those whom one might suppose his natural constituency was that he seemed truly to want to kill his opponents: in his prime he was the "baby-faced assassin" with the "dead eyes" and "deadpan" expression who once said, having knocked out an opponent named Ray Lampkin, that he hadn't trained for the fight—next time he would kill the man. (According to legend Durán once felled a horse with a single blow.) Sonny Liston was another champion lauded for his menace, so different in spirit from Floyd Patterson as to seem to belong to another subspecies; to watch Liston overcome Patterson in tapes of their fights in the early 1960s is to watch the defeat of "civilization" by something so elemental and primitive it cannot be named. Masculinity in these terms is strictly hierarchical—two men cannot occupy the same space at the same time.

At the present time twenty-year-old Mike Tyson, Cus D'Amato's much-vaunted protégé, is being groomed as the most dangerous man in the heavyweight division. He is spoken of with awe as a "young bull"; his strength is prodigious, at least as demonstrated against fairly hapless, stationary opponents; he enters the arena robeless—"I feel more like a warrior"—and gleaming with sweat. He does not even wear socks. His boxing model is not Muhammad Ali, the most brilliant heavyweight of modern times, but Rocky Marciano, graceless, heavy-footed, indomitable, the man with the massive right-hand punch who was willing to absorb five blows in the hope of landing one. It was after having broken Jesse Ferguson's nose in a recent match that Tyson told reporters that it was his strategy to try to drive the bone back into the brain . . .

The names of boxers! *Machismo* as sheer poetry.

Though we had, in another era, "Gentleman Jim" Corbett (world heavyweight champion, 1892–97); and the first black heavyweight champion, Jack Johnson (1908–15) called himself "Li'l Arthur" as a way of commenting playfully on his powerful physique and savage ring style. (Johnson was a white man's nightmare: the black man who mocked his white opponents as he humiliated them with his fists.) In more recent times we had "Sugar Ray" Robinson and his younger namesake "Sugar Ray" Leonard. And Tyrone Crawley, a thinking man's boxer, calls himself "The Butterfly." But for the most part a boxer's ring name is chosen to suggest something more ferocious: Jack Dempsey of Manassa, Colorado, was "The Manassa Mauler"; the formidable Harry Greb was "The Human Windmill"; Joe Louis was, of course, "The Brown Bomber"; Rocky Marciano, "The Brockton Blockbuster"; Jake LaMotta, "The Bronx Bull"; Tommy Jackson, "Hurricane" Jackson; Roberto Durán, "Hands of Stone" and "The Little Killer" variously. More recent are Ray "Boom-Boom" Mancini, Thomas "Hit-Man" Hearns, James "Hard Rock" Green, Al "Earthquake" Carter, Frank "The Animal" Fletcher, Donald "The Cobra" Curry, Aaron "The Hawk" Pryor, "Terrible" Tim Witherspoon, "Bonecrusher" Smith, Johnny "Bump City" Bumphus, Lonnie "Lightning" Smith, Barry "The Clones Cyclone" McGuigan, Gene "Mad Dog" Hatcher, Livingstone "Pit Bull" Bramble, Hector "Macho Man" Camacho. "Marvelous" Marvin Hagler changed his name legally to Marvelous Marvin Hagler before his fight with Thomas Hearns brought him to national prominence.

It was once said by José Torres that the *machismo* of boxing is a condition of poverty. But it is not, surely, a condition uniquely of poverty? Or even of adolescence? I think of it as the obverse of the feminine, the denial of the feminine-in-man that has its ambiguous attractions for all men, however "civilized." It is a remnant of another, earlier era when the physical being was primary and the warrior's masculinity its highest expression.

We fighters understand lies. What's a feint?
What's a left hook off the jab?
What's an opening? What's thinking one thing
and doing another . . . ?
—JOSÉ TORRES,
former light-heavyweight champion of the world

One of the primary things boxing is about is lying. It's about systematically cultivating a double personality: the self in society, the self in the ring. As the chess grandmaster channels his powerful aggressive impulses onto the game board, which is the world writ small, so the "born" boxer channels his strength into the ring, against the Opponent. And in the ring, if he is a good boxer and not a mere journeyman, he will cultivate yet another split personality, to thwart the Opponent's game plan vis-à-vis *him*. Boxers, like chess players, must think on their feet—must be able to improvise in mid-fight, so to speak.

(And surely it is championship chess, and not boxing, that is our most dangerous game—at least so far as psychological risk is concerned. Megalomania and psychosis frequently await the grand master when his extraordinary mental powers can no longer be discharged onto the chessboard.)

After his upset victory against WBC junior welterweight Billy Costello in August 1985 the virtually unknown "Lightning" Lonnie Smith told an interviewer for *The Ring* that his model for boxing was that of a chess game: boxing is a "game of control, and, as in chess, this control can radiate in circles *from* the center, or in circles *toward* the center . . . The entire action of a fight goes in a circle; it can be little circles in the middle of the ring or big circles along the ropes, but always a circle. The man who wins is the man who controls the action of the circle." Smith's ring style against Costello was so brazenly idiosyncratic—reminiscent at moments of both Muhammad Ali and Jersey Joe Walcott—that the hitherto undefeated Costello, known as a hard puncher, was totally demoralized, outclassed, outboxed. (As he was outfought some months later by a furious Alexis Arguello, who "retired" Costello from the ring.)

Cassius Clay / Muhammad Ali, that most controversial of champions, was primarily a brilliant ring strategist, a prodigy in his youth whose fast hands and feet made him virtually impossible for opponents to hit. What joy in the young Ali: in the inimitable arrogance of a heavyweight who danced about his puzzled opponents with his gloves at waist level, inviting them to hit him—to try it. (What joy, at any rate, in the Ali of films and tapes, even if in somber juxtaposition to the Ali of the present time, overweight, even puffy, his speech and reactions slowed by Parkinson's disease.) It was the young boxer's style when confronted with a "deadly" puncher like Sonny Liston to simply out-think and -maneuver him: never before, and never since, has a heavyweight performed in the ring with such style—an inimitable combination of intelligence, wit, grace, irreverence, cunning. So dazzlingly talented was Ali in his youth that it wasn't clear whether in fact he had what boxers call "heart"—the ability to keep fighting when one has been hurt. In later years, when Ali's speed was diminished, a new and more complex, one might say a greater, boxer emerged, as in the trilogy of fights with Joe Frazier, the first of which Ali lost.

Sugar Ray Leonard, the most charismatic of post-Ali boxers, cultivated a ring style that was a quicksilver balance of opposites, with an overlay of street-wise, playful arrogance (reminiscent, indeed, of Ali), and, for all Leonard's talent, it was only in his most arduous matches (with Hearns and Durán) that it became clear how intelligently ferocious a boxer he really was. Losing once to Durán, he could not lose a second time: his pride would not allow it. Just as pride would not allow Leonard to continue boxing when he suspected he had passed his peak. (Though at the time of this writing Leonard has publicly declared that he wants to return for one major match: *he* is the only man who knows how to beat Marvin Hagler. A matter of ego, Leonard says, as if we needed to be told.)

The self in society, the self in the ring. But there are many selves and there are of course many boxers—ranging from the shy, introverted, painfully inarticulate Johnny Owen (the Welsh bantamweight who died after a bout with Lupe Pintor in 1979) to the frequently manic Muhammad Ali in his prime (Ali whom Norman Mailer compared to a six-foot parrot who keeps screaming at you that he is the center of the stage: "Come here and get me, fool. You can't, 'cause you don't know who I am"); from the legendary bluster of John L. Sullivan to the relative modesty of Rocky Marciano and Floyd Patterson. (Patterson, the youngest man to win the heavyweight title, is said to have been a non-violent person who once helped an opponent pick up his mouthpiece from the canvas. "I don't like to see blood," Patterson explained. "It's different when I bleed, that doesn't bother me because I can't see it." He was no match physically or otherwise for the next heavyweight champion, Sonny Liston.) For every boxer with the reputation of a Roberto Durán there are surely a dozen who are simply "nice guys"—Ray Mancini, Milton McCory, Mark Breland, Gene Hatcher, among many others. Before he lost decisive matches and began the downward trajectory of his career the young Chicago middleweight John Collins was frequently promoted as a veritable split personality, a "Dr. Jekyll / Mr. Hyde" of the ring: the essential (and surely disingenuous) question being, How can a nice courteous young man like you turn so vicious in the ring? Collins's answer was straightforward enough: "When I'm in the ring I'm fighting for my life."

It might be theorized that fighting activates in certain people not only an adrenaline rush of exquisite pleasure but an atavistic self that, coupled with an instinctive sort of tissue-intelligence, a neurological swiftness unknown to "average" men and women, makes for the born fighter, the potentially great champion, the *unmistakably* gifted boxer. An outlaw or non-law self, given the showy accolade "killer instinct." (Though to speak of instinct is always to speak vaguely: for how can "instinct" be isolated from the confluence of factors—health, economic class, familial relations, sheer good or bad luck—that determine a life?) You know the boxer with the killer instinct when the crowd jumps to its feet in a ground swell of delirium in response to his assault against his opponent, no matter if the opponent is the favorite, a "nice guy" no one really wants to see seriously injured.

There is an instinct in our species to fight but is there an instinct to *kill?* And would a "born" killer have the discipline, let alone the moral integrity, to subordinate himself to boxing's rigors in order to exercise it? Surely there are easier ways: we read about them in the daily newspaper. That the fighter, like the crowd he embodies, responds excitedly to the sight of blood—"first blood" being a term from the days of the English Prize Ring—goes without saying; but there are often fight fans shouting for a match to be stopped at the very zenith of the action. My sense of the boxing crowd in a large arena like Madison Square Garden is that it resembles a massive wave containing counter-waves, counter-currents, isolated but bold voices that resist the greater motion toward ecstatic violence. These dissenters are severely critical of referees who allow fights to go on too long.

(I seem to recall my father urging a fight to be stopped: "It's over! It's over! What's the point!" Was it Marciano battering an opponent into submission, or Carmen Basilio? Kid Gavilan? A long time ago, and in our home, the bloody match broadcast over television, hence sanitized. One cannot really imagine the impact of blows on another man's head and body by way of the television screen in its eerily flattened dimensions . . .)

Granted these points, it is nonetheless true that the boxer who functions as a conduit through which the inchoate aggressions of the crowd are consummated will be a very popular boxer indeed. Not the conscientious "boxing" matches but the cheek-by-jowl brawls are likely to be warmly recalled in boxing legend: Dempsey-Firpo, Louis-Schmeling II, Zale-Graziano, Robinson-LaMotta, Pep-Saddler, Marciano-Charles, Ali-Frazier, most recently Hagler-Hearns. Sonny Liston occupies a position *sui generis* for the very truculence of his boxing persona—the air of unsmiling menace he presented to the Negro no less than the white world. (Liston was arrested nineteen times and served two prison terms, the second term for armed robbery.) It may be that former champion Larry Holmes saw himself in this role, the black man's black man empowered by sheer bitterness to give hurt where hurt is due. And, for a while, the Rastafarian Livingstone Bramble, whose vendetta with Ray Mancini seems to have sprung from an unmotivated ill will.

The only self-confessed murderer of boxing distinction seems to have been the welterweight champion Don Jordan (1958–60) who claimed to have been a hired assassin as a boy in his native Dominican Republic. "What's wrong with killing a human?" Jordan asked rhetorically in an interview. "The first time you kill someone, you throw up, you get sick as a dog . . . The second time, no feeling." According to his testimony Jordan killed or helped to kill more than thirty men in the Dominican Republic, without being caught. (He seems in fact to have been in the hire of the government.) After Jordan and his family moved to California he killed a man for "personal" reasons, for which crime he was sent to reform school, aged fourteen: "I burned a man like an animal . . . I staked him to the ground. I wired his hands and his arms, and I put paper around him and I burnt him like an animal. They said, 'You are mentally sick.' " In reform school Jordan was taught how to box: entered the Golden Gloves tournament and won all his matches, and eventually competed in the Olympics, where he did less well. Under the aegis of the Cosa Nostra he turned professional and his career, though meteoric, was short-lived.

In Jake LaMotta's autobiography *Raging Bull* LaMotta attributes his success as a boxer—he was middle-

weight champion briefly, 1949–51, but a popular fighter for many years—to the fact that he didn't care whether he was killed in the ring. For eleven years he mistakenly believed he had murdered a man in a robbery, and, unconfessed, yet guilty, wanting to be punished, LaMotta threw himself into boxing as much to be hurt as to hurt. His background parallels Rocky Graziano's—they were friends, as boys, in reform school—but his desperation was rather more intense than Graziano's (whose autobiography is entitled *Somebody Up There Likes Me:* a most optimistic assumption). LaMotta said in an interview: "I would fight anybody. I didn't care who they were. I even wanted to fight Joe Louis. I just didn't care . . . But that made me win. It gave me an aggression my opponents never saw before. They would hit me. I didn't care if I got hit." When LaMotta eventually learned that his victim had not died, however, his zest for boxing waned, and his career began its abrupt decline. By way of LaMotta's confession and the film based fragmentarily on it, *Raging Bull*, LaMotta has entered boxing folklore: he is the flashy gutter fighter whose integrity will allow him to throw only one fight (in an era in which fights were routinely thrown), done with such ironic disdain that the boxing commission suspends his license.

Traditionally, boxing is credited with changing the lives of ghetto-born or otherwise impoverished youths. It is impossible to gauge how many boxers have in fact risen from such beginnings but one might guess it to be about 99 percent—even at the present time. (Muhammad Ali is said to have been an exception in that his background was not one of desperate poverty: which helps to account, perhaps, for Ali's early boundless confidence.) Where tennis lessons were offered in some youth centers in the Detroit area, many years ago, boxing lessons were offered in Joe Louis's and Ray Robinson's neighborhood—of course. To what purpose would poor black boys learn tennis? La-Motta, Graziano, Patterson, Liston, Hector Camacho, Mike Tyson—all learned to box in captivity, so to speak. (Liston, a more advanced criminal than the others, began taking boxing lessons while serving his second term for armed robbery in the Missouri State Penitentiary.) Boxing is the moral equivalent of war of which, in a radically different context, William James spoke, and it has the virtue—how American, this virtue!—of making a good deal of money for its practitioners and promoters, not all of whom are white.

Indeed, one of the standard arguments for *not* abolishing boxing is in fact that it provides an outlet for the rage of disenfranchised youths, mainly black or Hispanic, who can make lives for themselves by way of fighting one another instead of fighting society.

The disputable term "killer instinct" was coined in reference to Jack Dempsey in his prime: in his famous early matches with Jess Willard, Georges Carpentier, Luis Firpo ("The Wild Bull of the Pampas"), and other lesser known boxers whom he savagely and conclusively beat. Has there ever been a fighter quite like the young Dempsey?—the very embodiment, it seems, of hunger, rage, the will to do hurt; the spirit of the Western frontier come East to win his fortune. The crudest of nightmare figures, Dempsey is gradually refined into an American myth of comforting dimensions. The killer in the ring becomes the New York *restaurateur*, a business success, "the gentlest of men."

Dempsey was the ninth of eleven children born to an impoverished Mormon sharecropper and itinerant railroad worker in Colorado who soon left home, bummed his way around the mining camps and small towns of the West, began fighting for money when he was hardly more than a boy. It was said in awe of Dempsey that his very sparring partners were in danger of being seriously injured— Dempsey didn't like to share the ring with anyone. If he remains the most spectacular (and most loved) champion in history it is partly because he fought when boxing rules were rather casual by our standards; when, for instance, a boxer was allowed to strike an opponent as he struggled to his feet—as in the bizarre Willard bout, and the yet more bizarre bout with Luis Firpo, set beside which present-day heavyweight matches like those of Holmes and Spinks are minuets. Where aggression has to be cultivated in some champion boxers (Tunney, for example) Dempsey's aggression was direct and natural: in the ring, he seems to have wanted to kill his opponent. The swiftness of his attack, his disdain for strategies of defense, endeared him to greatly aroused crowds who had never seen anything quite like him before.

(Dempsey's first title fight, in 1919, against the aging champion Jess Willard, was called at the time "pugilistic murder" and would certainly be stopped in the first round —in the first thirty seconds of the first round—today. Badly out of condition, heavier than the twenty-four-year-old Dempsey by seventy pounds, the thirty-seven-year-old Willard put up virtually no defense against the challenger. Though films of the match show an astonishing resilient, if not foolhardy, Willard picking himself up off the canvas repeatedly as Dempsey knocks him down, by the end of the fight Willard's jaw was broken, his cheekbone split, nose smashed, six teeth broken off at the gum, an eye was battered shut, much damage done to his lower body. Both boxers were covered in Willard's blood. Years later Dempsey's estranged manager Kearns confessed, perhaps fraudulently, that he had "loaded" Dempsey's gloves—treated his hand tape with a talcum substance that turned hard as concrete when wet.)

It was Dempsey's ring style—swift, pitiless, always direct and percussive—that changed American boxing forever. Even Jack Johnson appears stately by contrast.

So far as "killer instinct" is concerned Joe Louis was an anomaly, which no biography of his life—even the most recent, the meticulously researched *Champion—Joe Louis, Black Hero in White America* by Chris Mead—has ever quite explained. If, indeed, one can explain any of our motives, except in the most sweeping psychological and sociological terms. Louis was a modest and self-effacing man outside the ring, but, in the ring, a machine of sorts for hitting—so (apparently) emotionless that even sparring partners were spooked by him. "It's the eyes," one said. "They're blank and staring, always watching you. That blank look—that's what gets you down." Unlike his notorious predecessor Jack Johnson and his yet more notorious successor Muhammad Ali, Joe Louis was forced to live his "blackness" in secret, if at all; to be a *black* hero in *white* America at the time of Louis's coming-of-age cannot have been an easy task. Louis's deadpan expression and his killer's eyes were very likely aspects of the man's strategy rather than reliable gauges of his psyche. And his descent into mental imbalance—paranoia, in particular—in his later years was surely a consequence of the pressures he endured, if not an outsized, but poetically valid, response to the very real scrutiny of others focused upon him for decades.

One of the most controversial of boxing legends has to do with the death of Benny "Kid" Paret at the hands of Emile Griffith in a welterweight match in Madison Square Garden in 1962. According to the story Paret provoked Griffith at their weigh-in by calling him *maricón* (faggot), and was in effect killed by Griffith in the ring that night. Recalling the event years later Griffith said he was only following his trainer's instructions—to hit Paret, to hurt Paret, to keep punching Paret until the referee made him stop. By which time, as it turned out, Paret was virtually dead. (He died about ten days later.)

Though there are other boxing experts, present at the

match, who insist that Paret's death was accidental: it "just happened."

At the present time boxing matches are usually monitored by referees and ringside physicians with extreme caution: a recent match between welterweights Don Curry and James Green was stopped by the referee because Green, temporarily disabled, had lowered his gloves and *might have been hit;* a match between heavyweights Mike Weaver and Michael Dokes was stopped within two minutes of the first round, before the luckless Weaver had time to begin. With some exceptions—the Sandoval-Canizales and the Bramble-Crawley title fights come most immediately to mind—referees have been assuming ever greater authority in the ring so that it sometimes seems that the drama of boxing has begun to shift: not will X knock out his opponent, but will the referee stop the fight before he can do so. In the most violent fights the predominant image is that of the referee hovering at the periphery of the action, stepping in to embrace a weakened or defenseless man in a gesture of paternal solicitude. This image carries much emotional power—not so sensational as the killing blow but suggestive, perhaps, that the ethics of the ring have evolved to approximate the ethics of everyday life. It is as if, in mythical terms, brothers whose mysterious animosity has brought them to battle are saved —absolved of their warriors' enmity—by the wisdom of their father and protector. One came away from the eight-minute Hagler-Hearns fight with the vision of the dazed Hearns, on his feet but not fully conscious, saved by referee Richard Steele from what would have been serious injury, if not death—considering the extraordinary ferocity of Hagler's fighting that night, and the personal rage he seems to have brought to it. ("This was war," Hagler said.) The fight ends with Hearns in Steele's embrace: tragedy narrowly averted.

Of course there are many who disdain such developments. It's the *feminization* of the sport, they say.

I was never knocked out. I've been unconscious, but it's always been on my feet.
—FLOYD PATTERSON,
former heavyweight champion of the world

No American sport or activity has been so consistently and so passionately under attack as boxing, for "moral" as well as other reasons. And no American sport evokes so ambivalent a response in its defenders: when asked the familiar question "How can you watch . . . ?" the boxing *aficionado* really has no answer. He can talk about boxing only with others like himself.

In December 1984 the American Medical Association passed a resolution calling for the abolition of boxing

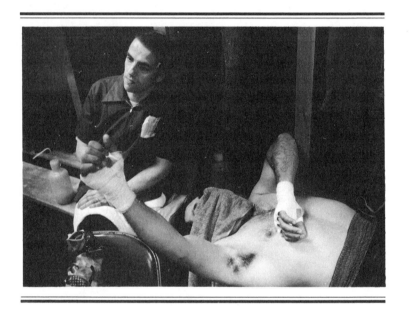

on the principle that while other sports involve as much, or even more, risk to life and health—the most dangerous sports being football, auto racing, hang gliding, mountain climbing, and ice hockey, with boxing in about seventh place—boxing is the only sport in which the objective is to cause injury: the brain is the target, the knockout the goal. In one study it was estimated that 87 percent of boxers suffer some degree of brain damage in their lifetimes, no matter the relative success of their careers. And there is the risk of serious eye injury as well. Equally disturbing, though less plausible, is sociological evidence that media attention focused on boxing has an immediate effect upon the homicide rate of the country. (According to sociologists David P. Phillips and John E. Hensley, the rate rises by an average of 12 percent in the days following a highly publicized fight, for the hypothetical reason that the fight "heavily rewards one person for inflicting violence on another and is at the opposite end of a continuum from a successfully prosecuted murder trial, which heavily punishes one person for inflicting physical violence on another.") Doubtful as these findings are in a culture in which television and movie violence has become routine fare, even for young children, it does seem likely that boxing as a phenomenon *sui generis* stimulates rather than resolves certain emotions. If boxing is akin to classic tragedy in its imitation of action and of life it cannot provide the *katharsis* of pity and terror of which Aristotle spoke.

The variegated history of boxing reform is very

likely as old as boxing itself. As I mentioned earlier, in the days of Pierce Egan's *Boxiana* the Prize Ring was in fact outlawed in England—though the aristocracy, including the Prince Regent, regularly attended matches. Boxing has been intermittently illegal in various parts of the United States and campaigns are frequently launched to ban it altogether. Like abortion it seems to arouse deep and divisive emotions. (Though activists who would outlaw abortion are not necessarily those who would outlaw boxing: puritanical instincts take unpredictable forms.) The relationship between boxing and poverty is acknowledged, but no one suggests that poverty be abolished as the most practical means of abolishing boxing. So frequently do young boxers claim they are in greater danger on the street than in the ring that one has to assume they are not exaggerating for the sake of credulous white reporters.

It is objected too that boxing as a sport is closely bound up with organized crime. Investigations on the federal and state level, over the decades, but most prominently in the fifties, have made the connection unmistakable, though the situation at any time is problematic. One wonders about "suspicious" decisions—are they fixed, or simply the consequence of judges' prejudices? As in Michael Spinks's second, highly controversial win over Larry Holmes, for instance; and the Wilfredo Gomez–Rocky Lockridge match of May 1985 (when judges gave a world junior-lightweight title to a Puerto Rican hometown favorite). And recent televised performances by former

Olympic Gold Medalists and their handpicked opponents have struck the eye of more than one observer as not entirely convincing . . .

Not long ago I saw a film of a long-forgotten fixed fight of Willie Pep's in which Pep allowed himself to be overcome by an underdog opponent: the great featherweight performed as a boxer-turned-actor might be expected to perform, with no excess of zeal or talent. It occurred to me that boxing is so refined, yet so raw a sport that no match can be successfully thrown; the senses simply pick up on what is not happening, what is being held back, as a sort of ironic subtext to what is actually taking place. You can run but you can't hide.

Not boxing in itself but the money surrounding it, the gambling in Las Vegas, Atlantic City, and elsewhere, is the problem, and a problem not likely to be solved. I have made an attempt to read the 135-page single-spaced document "Organized Crime in Boxing: Final Boxing Report of the State of New Jersey Commission of Investigation" of December 1985 and have come to the conclusion that the Commission, which has moved to abolish boxing in New Jersey, was wrongheaded in its initial approach: it should have been investigating organized crime in New Jersey, in which Atlantic City boxing/gambling figures. That the Commission would vote to abolish boxing altogether because of criminal connections suggests a naïveté shading into sheer vindictiveness: one would then be required to abolish funeral parlors, pizzerias, trucking firms, some labor unions. And if gamblers can't gamble on boxing they will simply gamble on football, basketball, baseball—as they already do.

Since boxing has become a multimillion-dollar business under the aegis of a few canny promoters—the most visible being Don King—it is not likely that it will be abolished, in any case. It would simply be driven underground, like abortion; or exiled to Mexico, Cuba, Canada, England, Ireland, Zaire . . . Boxing's history is one of such exigencies, fascinating for what they suggest of the compulsion of some men to fight and of others to be witnesses.

The 1896 heavyweight title match between Ruby Robert Fitzsimmons and Peter Maher, for instance, was outlawed everywhere in the States, so promoters staged it on an isolated sandbar in the Rio Grande River, four hundred miles from El Paso. (Can one imagine?—three hundred men made the arduous journey to witness what was surely one of the most disappointing title bouts in boxing history when Fitzsimmons knocked out Maher in ninety-five seconds.) During Jack Dempsey's prime in the 1920s boxing was outlawed in a number of states, like alcohol, and, like alcohol, seems to have aroused a hysterical public enthusiasm. Dempsey's notorious five minutes with the giant Argentinian Firpo was attended by eighty-five thousand people—most of whom could barely have seen the ring, let alone the boxers; both Dempsey's fights with Gene Tunney were attended by over a hundred thousand people—the first fought in a downpour during which rain fell in "blinding sheets" for forty minutes on both boxers and onlookers alike. Photographs of these events show jammed arenas with boxing rings like postage-sized altars at their centers, the boxers themselves no more than tiny, heraldic figures. To attend a Dempsey match was not to have seen a Dempsey match, but perhaps that was not the issue.

When Jack Johnson won the heavyweight title in 1908 he had to pursue the white champion Tommy Burns all the way to Australia to confront him. The "danger" of boxing at that time—and one of the reasons worried citizens wanted to abolish it—was that it might expose and humiliate white men in the ring. After Johnson's decisive victory over the White Hope contender Jim Jeffries there were in fact race riots and lynchings throughout the United States; even films of some of Johnson's fights were outlawed in many states. And because in recent decades boxing has become a sport in which black and Hispanic men have excelled it is particularly vulnerable to attack by white middle-class reformers (the AMA in particular) who show very little interest in lobbying against equally dangerous Establishment sports like football, auto racing, thoroughbred horse racing.

The late Nat Fleischer, boxing expert and founder of *The Ring* magazine, once estimated that tens of thousands of injuries have occurred in the ring since the start of modern boxing in the 1890s—by "modern" meaning the introduction of the rules of the Marquis of Queensberry requiring padded gloves, three-minute rounds, one minute's rest between rounds, continuous fighting during rounds. (The bare-knuckle era, despite its popular reputation for brutality, was far less dangerous for fighters—fists break more readily than heads.) Between 1945 and 1985 at least three hundred seventy boxers have died in the United States of injuries directly attributed to boxing. In addition to the infamous Griffith-Paret fight there have been a number of others given wide publicity: Sugar Ray Robinson killed a young boxer named Jimmy Doyle in 1947, for instance, while defending his welterweight title; Sugar Ramos won the featherweight title in 1963 by knocking out the champion Davey Moore, who never regained consciousness; Ray Mancini killed the South Korean Duk Koo-Kim in 1982; former featherweight champion Barry McGuigan killed the Nigerian "Young Ali" in 1983. After the death of Duk Koo-Kim the World Boxing Council shortened title bouts to twelve rounds. (The World Boxing Association retains fifteen. In the era of marathon fights, however—1892 to 1915—men often fought as many as one hundred rounds; the record is one hundred ten, in 1893, over a stupefying seven-hour period. The last scheduled forty-five-round championship fight was between the black title-holder Jack Johnson and his White Hope successor Willard in 1915: the match went twenty-six rounds beneath a blazing sun in Havana, Cuba, before Johnson collapsed.)

To say that the rate of death and injury in the ring is not extraordinary set beside the rates of other sports is to misread the nature of the criticism brought to bear against boxing (and not against other sports). Clearly, boxing's very image is repulsive to many people because it cannot be assimilated into what we wish to know about civilized man. In a technological society possessed of incalculably refined methods of mass destruction (consider how many times over both the United States and the Soviet Union have vaporized each other in fantasy) boxing's display of direct and unmitigated and seemingly natural aggression is too explicit to be tolerated.

Which returns us to the paradox of boxing: its obsessive appeal for many who find in it not only a spectacle involving sensational feats of physical skill but an emotional experience impossible to convey in words; an art form, as I've suggested, with no natural analogue in the arts. Of course it is primitive, too, as birth, death, and erotic love might be said to be primitive, and forces our reluctant acknowledgment that the most profound experiences of our lives are physical events—though we believe ourselves to be, and surely are, essentially spiritual beings.

I ain't never liked violence.
—*SUGAR RAY ROBINSON,*
former welterweight and
middleweight champion of the world

To the untrained eye most boxing matches appear not merely savage but mad. As the eye becomes trained, however, the spectator begins to see the complex patterns that underlie the "madness"; what seems to be merely confusing action is understood to be coherent and intelligent, frequently inspired. Even the spectator who dislikes violence in principle can come to admire highly skillful boxing—to admire it beyond all "sane" proportions. A brilliant boxing match, quicksilver in its motions, transpiring far more rapidly than the mind can absorb, can have the power that Emily Dickinson attributed to great poetry: you know it's great when it takes the top of your head off. (The physical imagery Dickinson employs is peculiarly apt in this context.)

This early impression—that boxing is "mad," or mimics the actions of madness—seems to me no less valid, however, for being, by degrees, substantially modi-

fied. It is never erased, never entirely forgotten or overcome; it simply sinks beneath the threshold of consciousness, as the most terrifying and heartrending of our lives' experiences sink beneath the level of consciousness by way of familiarity or deliberate suppression. So one knows, but does not (consciously) know, certain intransigent facts about the human condition. One does not (consciously) know, but one *knows*. All boxing fans, however accustomed to the sport, however many decades have been invested in their obsession, know that boxing is sheerly madness, for all its occasional beauty. That knowledge is our common bond and sometimes—dare it be uttered?—our common shame.

To watch boxing closely, and seriously, is to risk moments of what might be called animal panic—a sense not only that something very ugly is happening but that, by watching it, one is an accomplice. This awareness, or revelation, or weakness, or hairline split in one's cuticle of a self can come at any instant, unanticipated and unbidden; though of course it tends to sweep over the viewer when he is watching a really violent match. I feel it as vertigo—breathlessness—a repugnance beyond language: a sheerly physical loathing. That it is also, or even primarily, self-loathing goes without saying.

For boxing really isn't metaphor, it is the thing in itself. And my predilection for watching matches on tape, when the outcomes are known, doesn't alter the fact that, as the matches occurred, they occurred in the present tense, and for one time only. The rest is subterfuge—the intellectual's uneasy "control" of his material.

Impossible to see the old, early fights of Dempsey's and not to feel this *frisson* of dread, despite the poor quality of the films, the somewhat antic rhythms of the human figures. Or, I would guess, the trilogy of Zale-Graziano fights about which people speak in awe forty years later. For one man of my acquaintance it was a fight of Joe Louis's, against a long-forgotten opponent. For another, one of the "great" dirty matches of Willie Pep and Sandy Saddler—"little white perfection / and death in red plaid trunks" as the poet Philip Levine has written of that infamous duo. There was Duk Koo-Kim, there was Johnny Owen, in an earlier decade luckless Benny Paret, trapped in the ropes as referee Ruby Goldstein stood frozen, unable to interfere—

And Paret? Paret died on his feet. As he took those eighteen punches something happened to everyone who was in psychic range of the event. Some part of his death reached out to us. One felt it hover in the air. He was still standing in the ropes, trapped as he had been before, he gave some little half-smile of regret, as if he were saying, "I didn't know I was going to die just yet," and then, his head leaning back but still erect, his death came to breathe about him. He began to pass away. He went down more slowly than any fighter had ever gone down, he went down like a large ship which turns on end and slides second by second into its grave.

As he went down, the sound of Griffith's punches echoed
in the mind like a heavy ax in the distance chopping
into a wet log.
(NORMAN MAILER, *"Ten Thousand Words a Minute")*

For one friend of mine it was a bloody fight fought by the
lightweight contender Bobby Chacon that filled him with
horror—though, ironically, Chacon came back to win the
match (as Chacon was once apt to do). For another friend,
a fellow novelist, enamored of boxing since boyhood, it
was the Hagler-Hearns fight of 1985—he was frightened
by his own ecstatic participation in it.

At such times one thinks: What is happening? why
are we here? what does this mean? can't this be stopped?
My terror at seeing Floyd Patterson battered into insensibility by Sonny Liston was not assuaged by my rational
understanding that the event had taken place long ago
and that, in fact, Patterson is in fine health at the present
time, training an adopted son to box. (Liston of course has
been dead for years—he died of a heroin overdose, aged
thirty-eight, in "suspicious" circumstances.) More justified, perhaps, was my sickened sense that boxing is, simply, wrong, a mistake, an outlaw activity for some reason
under the protectorate of the law, when, a few weeks ago
in March 1986, I sat in the midst of a suddenly very quiet
closed-circuit television audience in a suburban Trenton
hall watching bantamweight Richie Sandoval as he lay flat
and unmoving on his back . . . very likely dead of a
savage beating the referee had not, for some reason,

stopped in time. My conviction was that anything was preferable to boxing, anything was preferable to seeing another minute of it, for instance standing outside in the parking lot for the remainder of the evening and staring at the stained asphalt . . .

A friend who is a sportswriter was horrified by the same fight. In a letter he spoke of his intermittent disgust for the sport he has been watching most of his life, and writing about for years: "It's all a bit like bad love—putting up with the pain, waiting for the sequel to the last good moment. And like bad love, there comes the point of being worn out, when the reward of the good moment doesn't seem worth all the trouble . . ."

Yet we don't give up on boxing, it isn't that easy. Perhaps it's like tasting blood. Or, more discreetly put, love commingled with hate is more powerful than love. Or hate.

The spectacle of human beings fighting each other for whatever reason, including, at certain well-publicized times, staggering sums of money, is enormously disturbing because it violates a taboo of our civilization. Many men and women, however they steel themselves, cannot watch a boxing match because they cannot allow themselves to see what it is they are seeing. One thinks helplessly, This can't be happening, even as, and usually quite routinely, it *is* happening. In this way boxing as a public spectacle is akin to pornography: in each case the spectator is made a voyeur, distanced, yet presumably intimately involved, in an event that is not supposed to be happening as it is happening. The pornographic "drama," though as fraudulent as professional wrestling, makes a claim for being about something absolutely serious, if not humanly profound: it is not so much about itself as about the violation of a taboo. That the taboo is spiritual rather than physical, or sexual—that our most valuable human experience, love, is being desecrated, parodied, mocked— is surely at the core of our culture's fascination with pornography. In another culture, undefined by spiritual-emotional values, pornography could not exist, for who would pay to see it?

The obvious difference between boxing and pornography is that boxing, unlike pornography, is not theatrical. It is not, except in instances so rare as to be irrelevant, rehearsed or simulated. Its violation of the taboo against violence ("Thou shalt not kill" in its primordial form) is open, explicit, ritualized, and, as I've said, *routine* —which gives boxing its uncanny air. Unlike pornography (and professional wrestling) it is altogether real: the blood shed, the damage suffered, the pain (usually suppressed or sublimated) are unfeigned. Not for hemophobics, boxing is a sport in which blood becomes quickly irrelevant. The experienced viewer understands that a boxer's bleeding face is probably the least of his worries, and may, in fact, mean nothing at all—one thinks of Rocky Marciano's garishly bloodied but always triumphant face, Marvin Hagler's forehead streaming blood even as he outfought Thomas Hearns. The severely bleeding boxer and his seconds are anxious not about his cut face but about the possibility of the fight being stopped, which means a TKO victory for the opponent. Recall Ray "Boom Boom" Mancini in his second match with Livingstone Bramble, in which he desperately tried to wipe away with his gloves blood pouring from inch-long cuts in his eyelids: twenty-seven stitches were needed to sew up the cuts afterward. (Bramble, pragmatic like all boxers, naturally worked Mancini's damaged eyes as frequently as he could. Of 674 blows struck by Bramble 255 struck him in the face.)

Just as the boxer is trained to fight until he can't go on, so he is trained, or is by nature equipped, to fight unconscious on his feet. The image is indelibly imprinted in my memory of the doomed South Korean lightweight Duk Koo-Kim struggling to rise from the canvas after a blow of Mancini's burst a blood vessel in his brain—as if his body possessed its own demonic will even at the threshold of death. It is said that Joe Louis, badly stunned by Max Schmeling in their first fight, fought unconscious for several rounds—his beautifully conditioned body performing its trained motions like clockwork. (And it was during this losing bout that Louis's prodigious talent for endurance, and therefore for great boxing, manifested itself.) So customary is this sort of "fearless" boxing that the behavior of heavyweight Jesse Ferguson in his February 1986 match with Mike Tyson—clinching, holding on to Tyson's gloves, refusing in effect to fight—struck the eye as unnatural when of course it was utterly natural, the way the average man would behave in so desperate a situation. But boxing is contrary to nature.

One of the paradoxes of boxing is that the viewer inhabits a consciousness so very different from that of the boxer as to suggest a counter-world. "Free" will, "sanity," "rationality"—our characteristic modes of consciousness —are irrelevant, if not detrimental, to boxing in its most extraordinary moments. Even as he disrobes himself ceremonially in the ring the great boxer must disrobe himself of both reason and instinct's caution as he prepares to fight.

Dustin Hoffman recalls a boxing match he had seen as a boy: as the triumphant boxer left the ring to pass up the aisle, an ecstatic fight fan, male, followed closely after him, wiping all he could of the sweat from the boxer's body onto himself.

An observer is struck by boxing's intense preoccupation with its own history; its continuous homage to a gallery of heroes—or are they saints? At Muhammad Ali's Deer Lake, Pennsylvania, training camp the names of heavyweight champions—Louis, Marciano, Liston, Patterson, et al.—were painted in white letters on massive iconographic boulders. "Jack Dempsey" named himself for the middleweight champion Jack Dempsey (1884–91 —known as Dempsey "The Nonpareil" because he outboxed every man he fought). "Sugar Ray" Leonard named himself boldly after "Sugar Ray" Robinson—an act of audacity that did not prove embarrassing. If Marvin Hagler shaves his head, the image of Rubin "Hurricane" Carter comes to mind, and, beyond him, that of Jack Johnson himself—the first and very likely the greatest of defiantly *black* boxers, whom Cassius Clay / Muhammad Ali admired as well. So frequently are a few names evoked— Dempsey, Louis, Marciano, Pep, Robinson—one might think these boxers were our contemporaries and not champions of eras long past.

If boxing exhausts most of its practitioners in a Darwinian struggle for survival like virtually no other, it so honors a very few, so enshrines them in the glamour of immortality, surely the danger is justified? As in any religion, present and past are magically one; Time, even death, are defeated. The dead immortals are always with us, not only their names and the hazy outlines of careers recalled, but individual bouts, moments when decisive punches were thrown and caught, the size of a boxer's fist, the measurement of his reach, his age when he began and when he retired, his record of wins, losses, draws. The uppercut Jack Johnson used against Stanley Ketchel in 1909—the famous Fitzsimmons "shift" of 1897 (when

Fitzsimmons defeated Gentleman Jim Corbett for the heavyweight title)—the wicked left hook with which Jack Dempsey caught a distracted Jack Sharkey in 1927—Rocky Marciano's several right-hand knockout punches—Cassius Clay's mystery punch in the first minute of the first round of his second match with Sonny Liston—the left hook of Joe Frazier that knocked Muhammad Ali on his back in the fifteenth round of their first fight: all are commemorated. The typical boxing writer's imagination is not so much stimulated by his subject as enflamed. Dream matches are routinely fantasized in which boxers of different eras meet one another—Marciano-Dempsey, Louis-Ali, Hagler-Robinson, the 1961 Sonny Liston and the 1973 George Foreman. Boxers of different weights are thrown together—how would Willie Pep or Benny Leonard or Roberto Durán have done against Joe Louis, *equipped with the necessary poundage?* Though preoccupation with past records is common to most sports there is something unusually intense about it in boxing, perhaps because, in boxing, the individual is so very alone, or seems so. Like the saint he gives the impression of having arrived at his redemption by unflagging solitary effort.

The boxing past exists in an uncannily real and vital relationship with the present. The dead are not dead, or not merely dead. When, for instance, Larry Holmes made his ill-advised attempt to equal Rocky Marciano's record (forty-nine wins, no losses) it seemed suddenly that Marciano was living again, his name and photograph in all the papers, interviews with his family published. Michael

Spinks resurrected not only Billy Conn, the light-heavy-weight champion who was defeated in a famous match by Joe Louis in 1941 (and again in 1946) but any number of other light-heavyweight champions who were defeated by heavyweight champions—Georges Carpentier, Tommy Loughran, Joey Maxim, the indefatigable Archie Moore. The spectacular first round of the Hagler-Hearns match provoked reminiscences of "the greatest first rounds of all time." (Number one remains Dempsey-Firpo, 1923.) *The Ring*'s Hall of Fame—to which controversial Jake La-Motta was only recently elected—corresponds to the pan-theon of saints elected by the Vatican except it is in fact more finely calibrated, its saints arranged under various groupings and subgroupings, and its balloting highly com-plex. (Indeed, no intellectual journal in the States is more scrupulously attentive to its history than this famous box-ing magazine, founded by Nat Fleischer in 1922, in which past, present, and a hypothesized future are tirelessly ex-amined, and in which one finds articles on such subjects as "The Greatest Disappointments in Ring History," "The Greatest Mismatches," "The Greatest Left Hooks," "When a Good Little Man *Did* Defeat a Good Big Man.")

It is as if by way of the most strenuous exigencies of the physical self a boxer can—sometimes—transcend the merely physical; he can, if he is lucky, be absolved of his mortality. The instinct is of course closely allied with the desire for fame and riches (those legendary champions with their purple Cadillacs!) but is not finally identical with it. If the boxing ring is an altar it is not an altar of sacrifice solely but one of consecration and redemption. Sometimes.

"... I am a sophomore at [an upstate New York SUNY campus] and when I'm at school I work out at a downtown gym 5 days a week. The gym is completely removed from the atmosphere of school in every way. Through boxing I manage to release aggression . . . I've yet to have my first amateur fight. My trainer says when I'm sparring I don't look like I want to hurt my man. 'You gotta want to hurt him, because he's sure going to hurt you.' I'm afraid my lack of bloodlust stems from a fear of going too far, physically and/or mentally. However far I push myself in the gym something in me is holding back . . .

"I have very little idea what it was that attracted me to boxing in the first place. No one in my immediate experience ever had the least interest in it. What started as a little fooling around at the Y soon turned into almost an obsession . . . Over Christmas break I had a bad experience I'd rather not repeat. The trainer gave me a break, said he'd let me train with the team for a while, and I wound up sparring the first night with a fellow who outmatched me pretty badly in experience. I took a 3-round beating, never letting him knock me down, but *taking plenty of punishment, mostly jabs that landed on or around my nose, which I was sure must be broken by the end of the second round. After practice the trainer told me I had a hell of a lot of heart. Don't blow your nose, he said, or your eyes will black, and be here tomorrow. Driving home I knew 'heart' meant crazy or stupid or both, but still the wave of elation I felt matched the fear and trepidation that came over me before I entered that ring . . . and afterwards anticipating facing my parents. I didn't leave the house for days after that, I became depressed and embarrassed, I thought that perhaps boxing wasn't worth it after all, maybe I couldn't cut it, and I was afraid I'd already lost whatever looks I had. My face swelled up to an unspeakably ugly apparition, and I carried two black eyes for months afterwards.*

"I took an introductory course to poetry last semester and through it I became convinced that the best way to convey my reasons for and feelings about boxing would be through poetry . . ."

—excerpts of letters to
the author from a young boxer

*If they cut my bald head open,
they will find one big boxing glove.
That's all I am. I live it.*
—MARVIN HAGLER

Though boxing has long been popular in many coun-
tries and under many forms of government, dicta-
torships no less than democracies, surely its popularity in
the States since the days of John L. Sullivan has a good
deal to do with what Americans honor as the spirit of the
individual—his "physical" spirit—in defiance of the
State. The remarkable rise of boxing in the 1920s in particular can be seen as a consequence of the diminution of
the individual vis-à-vis society; the gradual attrition of
personal freedom, will, and strength—"masculine," to be
sure, but not solely masculine. What more appropriate
hero for the times than the pitiless ex-barroom brawler
Jack Dempsey of Manassa, Colorado? Today, the "totali-
tarian" consciousness in the Eastern bloc of nations is
clearly a function of the state while in the Western bloc it
has come to seem a function of technology, if not history
—inexorable fate. How to master these ever more difficult
machines, how even to learn their language, when so
many of us are illiterate . . . The individual exists in his
physical supremacy, but does the individual matter?

In the magical space of the boxing ring so disturbing
a question has no claim. There as in no other public arena
does the individual as a unique physical being assert himself; there, for a dramatic if fleeting period of time, the
great world with its moral and political complexities, its
terrifying impersonality, ceases to exist. Men fighting one
another with only their fists and their cunning are all
contemporaries, all brothers, belonging to no historical

time. The crowd, borne along with them, belongs to no historical time. "He can run but he can't hide"—so said Joe Louis before his great fight with Conn in 1941. In the brightly lit ring, man is *in extremis*, performing an atavistic rite or *agon* for the mysterious solace of those who can participate only vicariously in such drama: the drama of life in the flesh. Boxing has become America's tragic theater.

ON MIKE TYSON

November 22, 1986. When twenty-year-old Mike Tyson enters the packed arena of the Las Vegas Hilton Convention Center, it is through a deafening wall of noise. A neutral observer would wonder: Is this young man already a champion?—a *great* champion? Of the nearly nine thousand people jammed into the arena—in seats as costly as $1,000 at ringside—virtually everyone has come in expectation of seeing not merely a heavyweight title fight that promises to be unusually dramatic but boxing history itself. If Tyson takes away the World Boxing Council heavyweight title held by thirty-three-year-old Trevor Berbick, as he has promised to do, he will become the youngest heavyweight champion in the sport's recorded history. He will fulfill the prophecy made by the late Cus D'Amato, his boxing trainer, mentor, and guardian, that he would one day break the record of another of D'Amato's heavyweight prodigies, Floyd Patterson, who won the title shortly before his twenty-second birthday in 1956.

Mike Tyson, a boy warrior, has become legendary, in a sense, before there is a legend to define him. And never has the collective will of a crowd—the very nearly palpable *wish* of a crowd—been more powerfully expressed than it is tonight in Las Vegas. With his much-publicized 27–0 record as a professional boxer, of which twenty-five victories are knockouts (fifteen in the first round, several within sixty seconds), with so much expectation centered upon him as the "new hope" of heavyweight boxing, Tyson recalls the young Jack Dempsey, who fought his most spectacular fights before wining the heavyweight title. Like Dempsey in the upward trajectory of his career, Tyson suggests a savagery only symbolically contained within the brightly illuminated elevated ring, with its referee, its resident physician, its scrupulously observed rules, regulations, customs, and rituals. Like Dempsey he has the power to galvanize crowds as if awakening in them the instinct not merely for raw aggression and the mysterious will to do hurt that resides, for better or worse, in the human soul, but for suggesting the incontestable *justice* of such an instinct: his is not the image of the Establishment-approved Olympic Gold Medalist, like Muhammad Ali or Sugar Ray Leonard (indeed, it is said in boxing circles that Tyson was cheated of a gold medal at the 1984 Summer Olympic Games by way of the politics of amateur boxing), but the image of the outsider, the psychic outlaw, the hungry young black contender for all that white America can give. In a weight division in which hard punching is the point, Tyson has acquired a reputation for being an awesome fighter, as much admired and feared among his coevals as Sonny Liston, George

Foreman, and Rocky Marciano were in their times: he has been called a "tank," a "young bull," a "killer," a "block of granite"; a force primitive and irresistible as nature. As one observer noted, there is something of a comic-book quality about Tyson's fights—the violence is so exaggerated it has a surrealist air. Opponents are propelled across the ring, fall insensible into the ropes, or, fully conscious, lose muscular control in their legs; they lie without moving for what seems a very long time. The violence may appear primitive and surrealist but it is thoughtfully administered: the result, as Tyson explains carefully in his soft, earnest, boyish voice, of punches thrown with a "bad intention in a vital area." Cus D'Amato was, among other things, a "master of anatomy."

Tyson himself has spoken of the phenomenon of Mike Tyson in gladiatorial terms: the warrior's vow to fight to the death if necessary precludes and makes irrelevant all merely personal motives, all conventional rationalizations for what he does. Boxing is his life, his vocation; his calling. The Roman boast of *munera sine missione* in the gladiatorial games—no mercy shown— would be perfectly logical to him. And so mesmerizing has the young boxer become in his scant eighteen months as a professional, his appearance in the ring tonight in Las Vegas, his mere physical *presence*, captivates the crowd's attention to the degree that the entrance of reigning WBC champion Trevor Berbick goes virtually unnoticed. Even the blazoning recorded music is abruptly and mysteriously silenced.

Mike Tyson—"Kid Dynamite" as he has lately been billed—exudes an air of tension, control, fierce concentration. At five feet eleven inches, he is short for a heavyweight and strikes the eye as shorter still; his 222¼-pound body is so sculpted in muscle it looks foreshortened, brutally compact. (Berbick, at 218½ pounds, stands six feet two inches—not a large man by today's heavyweight standards—and will have a daunting seven-inch reach advantage.) Indeed, Tyson is so muscular as to resemble a bodybuilder rather than a boxer, for whom upper-body flexibility is crucial; his neck measures an extraordinary nineteen inches—larger than any heavyweight champion's since the circus strongman Primo Carnera. His hair is trimmed savagely short, Dempsey-style, along the back and sides, as if it were done with a razor; he wears not a robe but a crude white terry-cloth pullover that looks as if he might have made it himself and, as usual, no socks—"I feel more like a warrior this way"; and though his managers Jim Jacobs and Bill Cayton will be fined $5,000 by the Nevada State Athletic Commission for the privilege, Tyson is wearing the black trunks that have become his trademark. (Trevor Berbick, who usually wears white, preempted black for *his* trunks —very likely because he resents the extraordinary prefight publicity Tyson has engendered and the humiliating fact that, though the young challenger has never met an opponent of Berbick's stature, he is a 3-to-1 favorite to win tonight.) Tyson remains the object of the crowd's rapt attention. He is pumped up, covered in sweat, ready to fight. Though this is the hour—the very moment—to which the past six years of his life have been subordinated, he gives no sign of nerves and will say, afterward, that he was "calm" and "relaxed" in the knowledge that he could not fail.

As he gives Tyson final instructions, his trainer, Kevin Rooney—himself a D'Amato protégé—touches foreheads with him and kisses him lightly on the cheek. (Strangers to boxing's eerie combination of violence and childlike affection are invariably startled by such gestures, as by the abruptness with which, after the final bell, boxers often embrace each other in mutual gratitude for the fight. But such behavior, as spontaneous as it is traditional, and as natural as it is apparently contradictory, lies at the very heart of boxing.) As soon as the bell sounds, opening round one, Tyson rushes out of his corner to bring the fight to Berbick. In these quicksilver seconds, when far more happens than the eye, let alone the verbalizing consciousness, can absorb, it is clear that Tyson is the stronger of the two, the more dominant; willful. He pushes forward unmindful of Berbick's greater age and experience; the fight is to be *his* fight. If boxing is as much a contest of psyches as of physical prowess, it is soon clear that Tyson, on the attack, throwing beautifully controlled punches, is the superior boxer; and he is fast —unexpectedly fast. "This kid don't let you do what you want to do," Berbick's trainer Angelo Dundee will say after the fight. "He created the pressure and my guy didn't react to the pressure. . . . He throws combinations I never

saw before. When have you seen a guy throw a right hand
to the kidney, come up the middle with an uppercut, then
throw a left hook. He throws punches . . . like a trigger."
(This in significant contrast to Tyson's less effective performances against José Ribalta in August 1986 and James
"Quick" Tillis in May: the improvement, in so brief a period of time, is remarkable.) For those of us who have
been watching preliminary bouts for the past two and a
half hours, including a perfectly controlled but lackluster
if not contemptuous performance by former WBC champion Pinklon Thomas, the quality of Tyson's fighting—
one might say Tyson's *being*—is profound. The impact of
certain of his body blows is felt in the farthest corners of
the arena; the intensity of his fighting is without parallel.
As an observer notes, Tyson's punches even sound different from other boxers' punches. In the ring, in the terrible
intensity of action, Tyson is both sui generis and as stylized as the heraldic, struggling figures painted by George
Bellows in such famous oils as "Stag at Sharkey's" and
"Dempsey and Firpo." It seems suddenly possible that,
as Cus D'Amato predicted, Tyson differs not merely in
degree but in kind from his fellow boxers.

Early in the second round, Tyson knocks Berbick to
the canvas with a powerful combination of blows, including a left hook; when Berbick manages to get gamely to
his feet he is knocked down a second time with a left
hook to the head—to be precise, to the right temple, a
"vital area." (As Tyson will say afterward, he had come to
"destroy" the champion: "Every punch had a murderous

intention.") Accompanied by the wild clamor of the crowd as by an exotic sort of music, Berbick struggles to his feet, his expression glazed like that of a man trapped in a dream; he lurches across the ring on wobbly legs, falls another time, onto the ropes, as if by a sheer effort of will gets up, staggers across the ring in the opposite direction, is precariously on his feet when the referee, Mills Lane, stops the fight. No more than nine seconds have passed since Tyson's blow but the sequence, in slow motion, has seemed much longer. . . . The nightmare image of a man struggling to retain consciousness and physical control before nine thousand witnesses is likely to linger in the memory: it is an image as inevitable in boxing as that of the ecstatic boxer with his gloved hands raised in triumph.

At two minutes thirty-five seconds of the second round, the fight is over and twenty-year-old Mike Tyson is the new WBC champion. "I am the heavyweight champion of the world," he tells the television audience, "and I will fight anybody in the world."

The post-Ali era has finally ended.

Boxing is our most controversial American sport, always, it seems, on the brink of being abolished. Its detractors speak of it in contempt as a "so-called 'sport,'" and surely their logic is correct: if "sport" means harmless play, boxing is not a sport; it is certainly not a game. But "sport" can signify a paradigm of life, a reduction of its complexities in terms of a single symbolic action—in this case its competitiveness, the cruelty of its Darwinian enterprise—defined and restrained by any number of rules, regulations, and customs: in which case boxing is probably, as the ex-heavyweight champion George Foreman has said, the sport to which all other sports aspire. It is the quintessential image of human struggle, masculine or otherwise, against not only other people but one's own divided self. Its kinship with Roman gladiatorial combat—in which defeated men usually died—is not historically accurate but poetically relevant. In his classic *Theory of the Leisure Class* (1899), Thorstein Veblen speaks of sport in general as "an expression of the barbarian temperament," and it is a commonplace assumption for many boxers, particularly for young boxers like Mike Tyson, that in the ring they are fighting for their lives. (As Tyson said excitedly, following the Berbick fight, "I refuse to get hurt, I refuse to get knocked down, I refuse to lose—I would have to be killed—carried out of the ring. I would not *be* hurt.")

It should be kept in mind, however, that for all its negative publicity, and the sinister glamour of certain of its excesses, boxing is not our most dangerous sport. It ranks in approximately seventh place, after football, Thoroughbred racing, sports car racing, mountain climbing, et al. (It is far less systematically violent than professional football, for instance, in which, in a single season, hundreds of players are likely to be fined for the willful infraction of rules.) And in a time of sports mania unparalleled in our history, boxing remains the only major sport accessible to what is piously called "underprivileged" youth—the others are Establishment-controlled, sealed off from penetration by men with the backgrounds of Larry Holmes, Hector Camacho, Marvin Hagler, Mike Tyson.

It has always been, in any case, from the days of bare-knuckle prizefighting to the present, the sport that people love to hate. Its image of men pitted against each other in man-to-man warfare is too stark, too extreme, to be assimilated into "civilized" society. "You're fighting, you're not playing the piano, you know," welterweight champion Fritzie Zivic once said.

"Yes, I'm fighting for my life in the ring," Mike Tyson tells me. And, "I love boxing." And, a little later, "Am I a born boxer? No—if I was, I'd be perfect."

In person Mike Tyson exudes the air of an intensely physical being; he is guarded, cautious in his speech, wary of strangers, unfailingly courteous. His intelligence expresses itself elliptically, as if through a mask—though not the death's-head mask of the ring that so intimidates opponents. No doubt the referee's classic admonition, "Protect yourself at all times!" rings in his ears in situations like this—an interview, one of numberless interviews, thrust upon him in the ever-burgeoning phenomenon of Fame. (It is difficult to believe Tyson will ever be fully—narcissistically—comfortable in his celebrity as Muhammad Ali and Sugar Ray Leonard are in theirs.)

Tyson is a young man, a phenomenon, one might

say, of paradoxical qualities: more complex, and more
self-analytical, than he has seemed willing, in public, to
acknowledge. With his boyish gap-toothed smile and his
earnest voice he has disarmed speculation about his future as a precocious titleholder by telling reporters repeatedly that his life is simple: "You wouldn't believe
how simple it is. I'm too young to worry about so many
things. I let them worry." (Meaning that his professional
affairs are handled—and handled, it would seem, with
consummate skill—by managers Jim Jacobs and Bill Cayton of Big Fights Inc. and trainer Kevin Rooney.) He
acquiesces to media descriptions of himself as a "boy
champion"; he speaks, not, it seems, disingenuously, of
being a "kid" whose career is a masterwork guided by
others—primarily, of course, by the late Cus D'Amato.
("Cus laid the groundwork for Mike's career," Jim Jacobs
tells me. "And when I say Cus laid the groundwork, I
mean he laid the groundwork—for Mike's entire future
career.") The young boxer's relationship to his handlers
and to his "family"—an intimate though not blood-related
constellation of men and women linked by way of
D'Amato—allows him the freedom-within-discipline of
the child prodigy in music whose teacher and parents
zealously protect him from the outside world. And it is
readily clear, speaking with Mike Tyson in the presence
of Jim and Loraine Jacobs (my interview was conducted in
the Jacobses' apartment in the East Forties, Manhattan,
surrounded by boxing memorabilia that includes an entire
wall of films and tapes), that he is fully aware of his good

fortune; he understands that his emotional-professional situation is close to unique in the notoriously unsentimental world of professional boxing. He is loved by his family and he loves them—it is that simple, and that enviable. If in one sense, like other star athletes of our time, Mike Tyson *is* a child, he is also a fully, even uncannily mature man—a twenty-year-old like no other I have ever encountered.

"I'm happy when I'm fighting. The day of the fight—leading up to it—I'm happy," he says. In his black wool-and-leather sweater, black brushed corduroy trousers, a jewel-studded gold bracelet on his wrist, Mike Tyson looks very different from the man who "destroyed" Trevor Berbick seven days ago in Las Vegas; very different from the iconographic photographs of him that have appeared in various publications, here and abroad. (The Japanese are much taken with Tyson: his photograph has been on the cover not only of sports magazines but of movie and general-interest magazines. How to explain his popularity there, where he has never visited? Tyson smiles and shrugs. "Who knows?") Loraine Jacobs shows me a remarkable photograph of Tyson by Ken Regan of Camera 5 in which, in his boxing trunks, eerily shadowed and outlined by light, Tyson looks like a statue, or a robot—a high-tech fantasy of sheerly masculine threat and aggression. I ask Tyson what he thinks of his image—does it seem strange to him, to be so detached from a "Mike Tyson" who both is and is not himself—and Tyson mur-

murs something vaguely philosophical, like, "What can you do?" Yet it is clear that he too is fascinated by the phenomenon of Tyson; he remarks, a little later, that it would be interesting if he could in some way be in the audience at one of his own fights, where the excitement is. In the ring, in the cynosure of action, the fighter does not experience himself; what appears to the crowd as an emotionally charged performance is coolly calibrated. If Tyson feels fear—which, he acknowledges, he does—he projects his fear onto the opponent, as Cus D'Amato instructed: but little emotion is ever visible on Mike Tyson's own face.

If Tyson is happy in the ring, unlike many boxers who come to dislike and dread their own life's work, it is perhaps because he hasn't been hurt; hasn't been seriously hit; has never met an opponent who was in any sense a match for him. (Do any exist? Right now? Tyson and his circle don't think so.) At the age of twenty he believes himself invulnerable, and who, watching him in action, would deny it? One of the fascinations of this new young titleholder is the air he exudes of "immortality" in the flesh—it is the fascination of a certain kind of innocence.

Asked after the Berbick fight why he is so concerned with establishing a record "that will never, ever be broken," Tyson said, "I want to be immortal! I want to live forever!" He was being funny, of course—he often is, making such pronouncements to the press. But he was also, of course, deadly serious.

Baptized Catholic, he no longer practices the faith; but believes, he says, in God. As for life after death— "When you're dead, that's it." He is quick to acknowledge the extraordinary good fortune, amounting very nearly to the miraculous, that has characterized his life beyond the age of twelve, when, as a particularly unhappy inmate of the Tryon School for Boys in Johnstown, New York, a juvenile detention facility to which he was sent after committing burglaries and robberies in the Brownsville section of Brooklyn, he was brought to the attention of the elderly Cus D'Amato—a man who, judging by the testimony of numerous observers, seems to have had the mystical qualities of a Zen Master. But Cus D'Amato was a boxing trainer par excellence who had already cultivated another juvenile delinquent, Floyd Patterson, into a prodigy-champion heavyweight in the 1950s and had discovered José Torres (world light-heavyweight champion 1965–66 and current head of the New York State Boxing Commission) as an amateur boxer in Puerto Rico. The story is that, having observed the untrained thirteen-year-old Tyson box a few rounds in the gym he ran above the police station in Catskill, New York, D'Amato said to a Tryon School boxing coach: "That's the heavyweight champion of the world. If he wants it, it's his."

This is the stuff of legend, of course. Yet it happens to be true. The precocious criminal-to-be—Tyson's earliest arrests were at the age of ten—is taken up by one of boxing history's greatest trainers; is released into

D'Amato's custody and, two years later, is officially
adopted by him; lives, trains, most importantly is nour-
ished, in Catskill, New York, in a fourteen-room house
shared by D'Amato and his sister-in-law, Camille Ewald
—far from the corrosive atmosphere of the black ghetto,
in which, judging from his record, the young Mike Tyson
would have been doomed. "Cus was my father but he was
more than a father," Tyson says. "You can have a father
and what does it mean?—it doesn't really mean anything.
Cus was my backbone. . . . He did everything for my best
interest. . . . We'd spend all our time together, talk about
things that, later on, would come back to me. Like about
character, and courage. Like the hero and the coward:
that the hero and the coward both feel the same thing, but
the hero uses his fear, projects it onto his opponent, while
the coward runs. It's the same thing, fear, but it's what
you do with it that matters." (Jim Jacobs tells me afterward that much of what Mike says is Cus D'Amato speaking; much of what *he* says is Cus D'Amato speaking.)

Quite apart from his genius as a boxing trainer,
D'Amato appears to have been a genius of a spiritual sort,
if "genius" is not an inappropriate term in this context.
Like a devoted religious elder he instilled in Tyson, and
no doubt in others of his young boxer acolytes, qualities
of an abstract nature: self-denial, discipline, will, integrity, independence, "character." It was D'Amato's belief
that a fighter's character is more important ultimately
than his skill: a perception proven, in the ring, only in
the most arduous of fights—one thinks of the virtually

Shakespearean struggles of the first Ali/Frazier match, the 1941 Louis/Conn match, the Leonard/Hearns. Most importantly, D'Amato instilled in Tyson that most invaluable and mysterious of gifts, an unwavering faith in himself. "He said I would be the youngest heavyweight in history," marvels Tyson. "And what he said turned out to be true. Cus knew it all along."

Jim Jacobs, D'Amato's devoted friend, a boxing manager of enormous reputation and prestige and the archivist of twenty-six thousand boxing films, says that D'Amato's word regarding Tyson's promise was enough for him: there was no one in the world whose judgment he trusted more than Cus D'Amato's. "When Cus told me that Mike Tyson was going to be heavyweight champion of the world, that's all I had to hear." So internalized is D'Amato's voice, and his instructions regarding the nurturing of the young heavyweight, Jacobs says that when he thinks about what he is doing, he has only to "press a button in my head and I can hear Cus talking to me. What I am doing is precisely and exactly what Cus told me to do."

If Tyson looked upon D'Amato as a father—Tyson's "real" father seems never to have figured in his life—it is evident that D'Amato looked upon Tyson as a son. In an interview for *People* shortly before his death, D'Amato told William Plummer that the boy meant "everything" to him. "If it weren't for him, I probably wouldn't be living today. See, I believe nature's a lot smarter than anybody thinks. During the course of a man's life he develops a lot of pleasures and people he cares about. Then nature takes them away one by one. It's her way of preparing you for death. See, I didn't have the pleasures any longer. My friends were gone, I didn't hear things, I didn't see things clearly, except in memory. . . . So I said I must be getting ready to die. Then Mike came along. The fact that he is here and is doing what he is doing gives me the motivation to stay alive." Though D'Amato died of pneumonia in November 1985, aged seventy-seven, approximately a year before Tyson became the youngest titleholder in heavyweight history, he seems to be alive, still, in Tyson's soul. One man's faith in another can go no further.

Yet it would be imprecise to say that Mike Tyson is D'Amato's creature solely. His initial social shyness masks a quick, restless intelligence; he is not without humor regarding even the vicissitudes of his early life. Of his years as a child criminal—during which time, as the youngest member of a gang, he was frequently entrusted with holding a gun during robberies—he has said, "Please don't think I was really bad. I used to rob and steal but other guys did worse things—they murdered people." At times Tyson lived on the Bedford-Stuyvesant streets, slept in abandoned buildings like a feral child. When he was arrested, aged eleven, and sent to the Tryon School for Boys, no one could have guessed how his life, ironically, had been saved. He was violent, depressed, mute; one of the most intractable of the "incorrigible" boys. When he broke loose it required several adult men to overpower him. One official recalls having seen him dragged away in handcuffs, to be locked in solitary confinement.

Mike Tyson's story reminded me of those legendary tales of abandoned children so particularly cherished by the European imagination—Kasper Hauser of Nürnberg, the "wild boy" of the Aveyron. Such tales appeal to our sense of wonder, mystery, and dread; and to our collective guilt. These children, invariably boys, are "natural" and "wild"; not precisely mute but lacking a language; wholly innocent of the rudiments of human social relations. They are homeless, parentless, nameless, "redeemable" only by way of the devotion of a teacher father—not unlike Tyson's Cus D'Amato. But even love is not enough to save the mysteriously doomed Kasper Hauser, whose story ends as abruptly and as tragically as it begins. And the "wild boy" of the Aveyron loses the freshness of his soul even as he acquires the skills of language and social intercourse.

There is nothing nostalgic, however, about Tyson's feelings for his past. Many of his boyhood friends are in jail or dead; both his parents are deceased; he has a sister and a brother, both older, with whom he appears to be on friendly but not intimate terms. If he returns to his old neighborhood it is as a visitor of conspicuous dimensions: a hero, a "boy champion," a *Sports Illustrated* cover in the flesh. Like Joe Louis, Sugar Ray Robinson, Larry Holmes, et al., Mike Tyson has become a model of success for "ghetto youth," though his personal code of conduct, his remarkably assured sense of himself, owes nothing at all to the ghetto. He is trained, managed, and surrounded, to an unusual degree, by white men, and though he cannot be said to be a white man's black man he is surely not a black man's black man in the style of, for instance, Muhammad Ali (whose visit to Tyson's grammar school in Brooklyn made a powerful impression on him at the age of ten). Indeed, it might be said that Mike Tyson will be the first heavyweight boxer in America to transcend issues of race—a feat laudable or troubling, depending upon one's perspective. (In the light of which, a proposed match between Tyson and the zealously over-promoted "White Hope" candidate Gerry Cooney would have interesting consequences: allegiances are likely not to break down along cursory color lines.)

He will do what he can, Tyson says, to promote blacks, but he does not intend to become involved in politics. He will visit schools, make public appearances, do anti-drug commercials for the FBI and the State of New York. If his replies to questions about black consciousness—its literature, art, history—are rather vague, it should be said that his replies to most questions that deal with culture in a larger sense are vague. Tyson dropped out of Catskill High School in his senior year—"I hated it there"—to concentrate on his amateur boxing in clubs and Golden Gloves competitions under the tutelage of D'Amato; and at this point his formal education, such as it was, seems to have ended. He has virtually no interest in music—"I could live without music." He shrugs aside queries about art, dance, literature; his reading is limited to boxing books and magazines. With Jim Jacobs's library of twenty-six thousand fight films at his disposal he watches old fights with an almost scholarly passion— surely this is unusual, in a practitioner? (Jim Jacobs assures me it is.) For entertainment Tyson watches videos of karate movies, horror movies, occasionally even children's cartoons: no serious dramas, and no movies about the lives of fictionalized boxers. I am spared asking him the obligatory question about the preposterous *Rocky* movies.

It should not be assumed, on the evidence of the above, that Mike Tyson is not intelligent; or that he is intellectually limited. On the contrary, I sensed in him the prodigy's instinctive husbanding of the self: he dares not allow his imagination freedom in areas only peripheral to the cultivation of his talent. Because he is an unusually sensitive person—sensitive to others' feelings, not merely to his own—he does not want to be forced to expend himself in feeling, or in thinking; except of course on his own terms. The awareness of life's tragic ambiguity that serious art provides—the perception, as Henry James describes it in the preface to *What Maisie Knew*, that no themes are so human "as those that reflect for us, out of the confusion of life, the close connection of bliss and bale, of the things that help with the things that hurt, so dangling before us for ever that bright hard medal, of so strange an alloy, one face of which is somebody's right

and ease and the other somebody's pain and wrong"—
would be disastrous for the warrior boxer. When, the
story goes, Alexis Arguello (the great champion of the
featherweight, junior lightweight, and lightweight divisions) met Roberto Durán (the great champion of the
lightweight and welterweight divisions) and proffered his
hand to shake, Durán backed away and screamed, "Get
away! You're crazy! I'm not your friend!" To acknowledge
friendship, let alone brotherhood, always makes it difficult to kill—or to provide for spectators the extraordinary
mimicry of killing that boxing of the quality of Mike
Tyson's involves. Life is real and painful, and steeped in
ambiguity; in the boxing ring there is either/or. Either
you win, or you lose.

The brilliant boxer is an artist, albeit in an art not
readily comprehensible, or palatable, to most observers.
The instruments of his art are his own and his opponent's
bodies. That it is, in a sense, a contemplative art—
contemplated, dreamt-of, for weeks, months, even years
before it is executed—is a proposition important to understand if one is to understand the boxer. ("It's a lonely
sport," Mike Tyson, who is surrounded by people who
love him, says.) Obsession is not greatness but greatness
is obsession, so it is no accident that, in his ambition to
be not only the youngest titleholder in heavyweight history but (I would guess) the greatest titleholder of all
time, Tyson is always, in a spiritual sense, in training.
His admiration for past boxers—Stanley Ketchel, Jack
Dempsey, Henry Armstrong, Kid Chocolate—and, not

least, Roberto Durán, of whom he speaks with genuine awe—is the admiration of the shrewd apprentice for his elders, not necessarily his betters. When I ask Tyson to assess his heavyweight contemporaries, men he will be meeting in the ring in the next few years, he again becomes purposefully vague, saying he doesn't think too much about them: "That would drive me crazy." Pinklon Thomas, Gerry Cooney, Carl Williams, Tyrell Biggs, Bert Cooper—he'd rather change the subject. And this instinct too is correct: the boxer must concentrate upon his opponents one by one, each in turn: in the collective, they cannot be granted existence. I am reminded of a diary entry of Virginia Woolf's to the effect that she does not dare read her serious rivals. "Do I instinctively keep my mind from analysing, which would impair its creativeness? . . . No creative writer can swallow another contemporary. The reception of living work is too coarse and partial if you're doing the same thing yourself" (20 April 1935).

Similarly, Tyson does not want to think overmuch about fatal accidents in the ring. He takes it for granted that *he* will not, indeed cannot, be hurt—"I'm too good for that to happen"; on the subject of an opponent's fate at his hands he is matter-of-fact and pragmatic. He is a boxer, he does his job—throwing punches until his opponent is defeated. If, as in the infamous Griffith-Paret match of 1962, in which Paret, trapped in the ropes, was struck eighteen unanswered blows by Griffith, death does occur, that is no one's fault: it can be said to be an accident. "Each of you takes the same chance, getting into the ring," Tyson says in his soft, considered, alternately slow and hurried voice—one of the voices, perhaps, of Cus D'Amato. "That you might die. It *might* happen."

I ask Tyson what he was thinking when the stricken Berbick tried to get to his feet and he says quickly, "I hoped he wasn't hurt," and adds, "It was a deliberate punch, to the head—a bad intention in a vital area." The anatomical areas Tyson has been taught to strike with his sledgehammer blows include the liver, the kidneys, the heart, and, as in Berbick's case, a certain spot on the temple which, if struck hard enough, will cause a man to drop immediately to the canvas. He will be fully conscious, as Berbick was, but paralyzed. Helpless. Down for the count.

And Tyson is confident that he himself cannot be hurt—in any serious, permanent way?

"That's right. I can't be. I'm too good."

Following the accidental death of one of the Flying Wallendas some years ago, a surviving member of the family of famous aerial-trapeze performers told the press that none of them had any intention of quitting. "All of life," he said, "is just getting through the time between acts."

So too with the fighter who loves to fight; the man whose identity is so closely bound up with the ring that it might be said he has none, publicly speaking, outside it. His creative work is done only in the ring, and only at certain designated times. Taped, it becomes permanent;

it *is* himself—or all that posterity will know of him.

The extraordinary upward trajectory of Mike Tyson's career—twenty-eight professional fights in eighteen months—has been the result of discipline and concentration so fierce as to resemble monastic devotion. Now that he is a titleholder, and a celebrity, and no longer a hungry young contender, Tyson's sense of himself has irrevocably altered; though he has yet to unify the heavyweight title—to do so, he will have to beat "Bonecrusher" Smith for the WBA title and the elusive Michael Spinks for the IBF title—he is already being called, and, in excited moments, calls himself, the heavyweight champion of the world. He has outdistanced his contemporaries—the new young generation of boxers that includes such Olympic Gold Medalists as Tyrell Biggs, Mark Breland, Paul Gonzales, Meldrick Taylor, and Pernell Whittaker; he is the first among them to win not only a title but enormous popular success. "When I was a kid I wanted to be famous—I wanted to be somebody," Mike Tyson says. And: "If someone right now is going to be famous, I'm glad it's me." But fame and the rewards of fame are, in a very real sense, the counterworld of the boxer's training: they represent all that must be repressed in the service of the boxer's real, as opposed to his merely public, career. When boxers retire it is primarily because of the terrible rigors of training, not the risks of defeat, injury, or even death in the ring. (The boxer who is generally credited with having trained hardest is Rocky Marciano, who commonly spent upward of two months preparing for a fight.

And when Marciano decided to retire, undefeated, at the age of thirty-three, it was because the sacrifices of the training camp outweighed the rewards of celebrity: "No kind of money can make me fight again," Marciano said.) The existential experience of the fight itself—spectacular, amplified, recorded in its every minute detail—is not only the culmination of the formidable training period but, in its very flowering, or fruition, it presents the boxer-as-performer to the world. Very likely this physical expenditure of the self (Tyson typically refers to it as "matching my boxing skills against my opponent's"), this bedrock of what's real, casts the remainder of life into a light difficult to assess. Life outside the ring is real enough—yet is it *really* real? Not public display as such but the joy of the body in its straining to the very limits of ingenuity and endurance underlies the motive for such feats of physical prowess as championship boxing or aerial-trapeze work. The performer is rewarded by his performance as an end in itself; he becomes addicted, as who would not, to his very adrenaline. *All of life is just getting through the time between acts.*

Since Mike Tyson is a young man gifted with a highly refined sense of irony, if not a sense of the absurd, it cannot have escaped his attention that, much of the time, in public places like the expensive midtown restaurant in which our party has dinner following the interview, or the reception two weeks later in a private suite in Madison Square Garden before the Witherspoon-Smith elimination match, he is likely to be the only black in attendance. He is likely to be the youngest person in attendance, and the only man not dressed in a suit and tie. Above all he is likely to be the only person with a gold tooth and a homemade tattoo ("Mike" on his right bicep); and the only person who, not many years before, was so violent and uncontrollable ("I went berserk sometimes") he had to be forcibly restrained. But when I mention some of this to a fellow guest at the Garden reception the man looks at me as if I have said something not only bizarre but distasteful. "I doubt that Mike thinks in those terms," he says. Not even that Tyson *is* the only black in this gathering of well-to-do white people, an observation that would appear to be simple fact? But no, I am assured: "Mike Tyson doesn't think in those terms."

Following a brief speech by the gentleman who runs Madison Square Garden, Tyson is presented with a ceremonial gift: a glass paperweight apple symbolizing New York City. He is photographed, he smiles genially, expresses his thanks for the paperweight, stands looking at it, for a moment, with a bemused expression. When, afterward, I ask Tyson how he likes being a celebrity—since, after all, he wanted to be famous—he says, "It's okay." Then: "Most of the time these things drive me crazy." I observe that he has learned to smile very nicely for photographers, and he responds with a violent parody of a celebrity smile: a death's-head grimace that is fierce, funny, self-mocking, inspired.

Four weeks later, still being photographed—this time by photographers for two magazines simultaneously —Tyson is back in training in Catskill, New York, in a third-floor walk-up gym above Catskill Police Headquarters on main Street. The gym is small, well-weathered, romantically shabby; owned and operated by the city of Catskill but leased for $1 a year to the Cus D'Amato Memorial Boxing Club, a nonprofit organization. In the spareness of the gym's equipment as in the sentiment that so clearly accrues to its homeliest features, it is the very antithesis of today's high-tech high-gloss athletic clubs. It contains only a single ring and a few punching bags; its ceiling is high and blistered, its lights antiquated. Its peeling walls are covered with newspaper clippings, announcements of the Catskill Boxing Club, photographs and posters of great champions (Louis, Walcott, Charles, Marciano, Patterson, et al.), reproductions of magazine covers. Mike Tyson's entire career is recorded here, in miniature, and, beneath the legend WE MOURN HIS PASSING, there are numerous clippings and photographs pertaining to the late Cus D'Amato, who once presided over the Boxing Club. Tyson prefers this gym to any other, naturally: it was here he began training, aged thirteen, and here that D'Amato's spirit still resounds. The gym is as indelibly imprinted in Tyson's imagination as any place on earth, and one must suppose that his prodigious youthful success has consecrated it in turn.

No athletes train more rigorously than boxers, and no present-day boxer is more serious about his training than Mike Tyson. Indeed, for the first eighteen months of his career he seems to have kept in condition more or less as the legendary Harry Greb did—by fighting virtually all the time. Today Tyson has done his morning roadwork— "three to five miles; I like it then 'cause I'm alone"—and is now going through the exercises that constitute "preliminary" training. (In Las Vegas he will work with at least five sparring partners. As Jim Jacobs explains, the sparring partners need time to recover.) Dressed in a black leotard and blowsy white trunks he moves from "work" station to station, closely attended by his trainer, Rooney, whom he clearly respects, and for whom he feels a good deal of affection, perhaps, at least in part, because Rooney is himself a D'Amato protégé—a welterweight who once boxed on the U.S. Boxing Team—and even shared one or two cards with Tyson, when he was already Tyson's trainer.

The drills are fierce and demand more concentration, strength, and sheer physical endurance than any fight Tyson has yet fought. Rooney has set a timer made up of two bulbs, red and green, to monitor each drill, the red telling Tyson to pause, the latter to resume. First he jumps rope, as if in a kind of trance, the rope moving too swiftly to be seen; the spectacle of a man of Tyson's build, so light on his feet, so seemingly *weightless*, has a preternatural quality. Next the heavy bag: Rooney wraps his hands with white tape, Tyson puts on gloves, pushes the bag with his left, then pummels it with combinations as it swings back to him. Rooney stands close and after each flurry the two confer, even as the heavy bag still swings treacherously in and around them. As he launches his hooks Tyson leaps from point to laterial point with extraordinary agility—as if his upper body remains stationary while his lower body moves in sharp angles out of which solidly anchored punches are shot. These are blows of such daunting power it is difficult to comprehend how they could be absorbed by any human being... any fellow creature of flesh, bone, and blood.

Rooney is game to try, at least for a while, wearing padded mitts over his hands and forearms; then they move on to the "slip" bag, where Tyson bobs and weaves, eluding his invisible opponent's best-aimed blows to the head. Last, the speed bag. In the blurred and confusing action of a fight it is not so readily clear, as it is in the gym, that Tyson's relative shortness (he is considered a "little" heavyweight) is really to his advantage. Most of his opponents are taller than he, if not invariably heavier, so that they are obliged to punch at a downward angle, utilizing only their shoulder and arm muscles; while Tyson can punch upward, utilizing not only his shoulder and arm muscles but his leg muscles as well—and these muscles are massive. By crouching, he can make himself shorter, and yet more elusive. (As Jim Jacobs has explained, "People speak of a 'height advantage' when what they're really referring to is a 'height disadvantage.' If a boxer is good, and shorter than his opponent, the advantage is his, and not his opponent's. The same thing holds true with the fallacy of the 'reach advantage'—a boxer has

a 'reach advantage' only if he is superior to his opponent.") But the strangest, most dazzling thing about
Tyson's boxing style is really his speed: his incredible
speed. How, one wonders, can he do it? Weighing what
he does, and built as he is? And will he be able to keep it
up, in the years to come?

"Eat, sleep, and train," says Kevin Rooney. "Mike
loves to train."

But: "I'm tired," Tyson says several times, in a soft,
nearly inaudible voice. (He is still being photographed.)
In his black leotard, towel in hand, he is literally
drenched in sweat; exuding sweat like tears. One can see
how much easier fighting has been for him than the regi-
men Rooney has devised—so many of Tyson's fights have
lasted less than five minutes, against opponents lacking
the skill to so much as raise a welt on his face, or cause
him to breathe hard. And this training session is only the
beginning—on February 3 he leaves for Las Vegas and
four weeks of "intensive" training.

He showers, dresses, reappears in jeans, a white
tuniclike jacket, stylish tweed cap, brilliantly white
Gucci sports shoes—surely the only shoes of their kind in
Catskill, New York? When we're photographed together
in the corner of the ring he complains in my ear of the
hours he has endured that day alone, facing cameras:
"You can't believe it! On and on!" Fame's best-kept
secret—its soul-numbing boredom—has begun to impress
itself upon Mike Tyson.

Catskill, New York, is a small town of less than six

thousand inhabitants. Its well-kept wood-frame houses have that prewar American look so immediately appealing to some of us—the very architecture of nostalgia. Like Main Street, with its Newberry's Five-and-Dime, Joe's Food Market, Purina Chows, the Town of Catskill town hall a storefront facing the police station, and the village offices—clerk, treasurer, tax collector—in the same building as the Catskill Boxing Club. Parking here is five cents an hour.

Mike Tyson lives two or three miles away, in one of the largest and most attractive houses in town, the home of Mrs. Camille Ewald, Cus D'Amato's sister-in-law. The house is at the end of an unpaved, seemingly private road, immaculately kept outside and in, yet comfortable—"I've lived here for seven years now," Tyson says proudly. He leads me through a kitchen and through a parlor room gleaming with trophies he doesn't acknowledge and we sit at one end of an immense living room while, from varying distances, a photographer (from Japan) continues to take candid shots of him he doesn't acknowledge either.

Life in Catskill is quiet and nourishingly routine: up at 6 A.M., to bed at 9 P.M. Daily workouts at the gym with Rooney; a diet of meat, vegetables, pasta, fruit juice—never any alcohol or caffeine; a modicum, in this semirural environment, of monastic calm. But there are numerous distractions: last week Tyson addressed a junior high school in New York City, under the auspices of the Drug Enforcement Agency, and tomorrow he is due to fly to Jamaica for a boxing banquet at which, however improbably, Don King is going to be given a humanitarian award—"But I'm not going; I'm too tired." He speaks soberly of the responsibility of celebrity; the fact that fame requires, of its conscientious recipients, a degree of civic servitude. The awareness weighs upon him almost visibly.

With equal sobriety, and a mysterious conviction, Tyson goes on to say that friends, certain friends—"some of them the ones you like best"—can't be relied upon. "They want to be your friend, or say they do, then the least thing that goes wrong—" He makes a dismissive gesture. "They're gone." I suggest that this can't be the case with people he has known a long time, before he became famous, like Jim and Loraine Jacobs, and Tyson's face brightens. The Jacobses will always be his friends, he agrees. "No matter if I lost every fight from now on, if I was knocked down, knocked out—they'd always be my friends. That's right." He seems momentarily cheered.

Tyson's prize possession in Catskill is a young female dog of an exquisite Chinese breed, Shar-Pei, with an appealingly ugly pug face, rippling creases of flesh on its back, a body wildly animated by affection. He'd always wanted one of these dogs, Tyson says, but hadn't been able to afford it until now. "In China they were bred to hunt wild boars—that's why they have those wrinkles on their backs," he explains. "So when the boar bit into them they could twist around to keep on attacking." As Tyson speaks fondly of this uniquely evolved creature I am reminded of Tyson's own ring strategy—his agility at slipping an opponent's blows, ducking or leaning far to one side, then returning with perfect leverage and timing to counterpunch, often with his devastating right upper-cut. The "little" warrior dramatically overcoming the larger. . . . He loves this dog, he says. For the first time today he looks genuinely happy.

On our way out of the house, Tyson shows me the dining room in which he ate so many meals with Cus D'Amato. The room is handsomely furnished, flooded with sunshine on this clear winter day. "Cus sat here," Tyson says, indicating the head of the table, "—and I sat here. By his side."

When Santayana said that another world to live in is what we mean by religion, he could hardly have foreseen how his remark might apply to the sports mania of our time; to the extraordinary passion, amounting very nearly to religious fervor and ecstasy, millions of Americans commonly experience in regard to sport. For these people —the majority of them men—sports has become the "other world," preempting, at times, their interest in "this" world: their own lives, work, families, official religions.

Set beside the media-promoted athletes of our time and the iconography of their success, the average man knows himself merely average. In a fiercely competitive sport like boxing, whose pyramid may appear democrati-cally broad at the base but is brutally minuscule at the top, to be even less than great is to fail. A champion boxer, hit by an opponent and hit hard, may realize the total collapse of his career in less time than it takes to read this sentence. Boxing is not to be seized as a metaphor for life, but its swift and sometimes irremediable reversals of fortune starkly parallel those of life, and the blow we never saw coming—invariably, in the ring, the knockout blow—is the one that decides our fate. Boxing's dark fascination is as much with failure, and the courage to forbear failure, as it is with triumph. Two men climb into a ring from which, in symbolic terms, only one climbs out.

After the Berbick fight Tyson told reporters he'd wanted to break Berbick's eardrum. "I try to catch my opponent on the tip of the nose," he was quoted after his February 1986 fight with the hapless Jesse Ferguson, whose nose was broken in the match, "because I want to punch the bone into the brain." Tyson's language is as direct and brutal as his ring style, yet, as more than one observer has noted, strangely disarming—there is no air of menace, or sadism, or boastfulness in what he says: only the truth. For these reasons Mike Tyson demonstrates more forcefully than most boxers the paradox at the heart of this controversial sport. That he is "soft-spoken," "courteous," "sensitive," clearly thoughtful, intelligent, introspective; yet at the same time—or nearly the same time—he is a "killer" in the ring. That he is one of the most warmly affectionate persons, yet at the same time— or nearly—a machine for hitting "sledgehammer" blows. How is it possible? one asks. And why? Boxing makes graphically clear the somber fact that the same individual can be thoroughly "civilized" and "barbaric" depending upon the context of his performance. "I'm a boxer," Tyson says. "I'm a warrior. Doing my job." Murder, a legal offense, cannot occur in the ring. Any opponent who agrees to fight a man of Tyson's unique powers must know what he is doing—and, as Tyson believes, each boxer takes the same chance: matching his skills against those of his opponent.

The fictive text against which boxing is enacted has to do with the protection of human life; the sacramental vision of life. *Thou shalt not kill* (or maim, wound, cause to suffer injury) and *Do unto others as you would have them do unto you* are the implicit injunctions against which the spectacle unfolds and out of which its energies arise. The injunctions are, for the duration of the "game," denied, or repressed, or exploited. Far from being primitive, boxing is perhaps the most highly regulated and ritualistic of sports, so qualified by rules, customs, and unspoken traditions that it stands in a unique, albeit teasing, relationship to the extremes of human emotion: rage, despair, terror, cruelty, ecstasy. It is an art, as I've suggested, in which the human body itself is the instrument; its relationship to unmediated violence is that of a musical composition to mere noise. There may be a family kinship between Bach and aleatory "music," but the kinship is hardly the most significant thing about either.

But what, one wonders, is the purpose of so extreme an art?—can it have a purpose? Why do some men give themselves to it so totally, while others, as spectators, stare in rapt fascination—and pay so much money for the privilege of doing so?

Wallace Stevens's insight that the death of Satan was a tragedy for the imagination has no validity in terms of the curious aesthetic phenomenon that is professional boxing. In the boxing ring, elevated, harshly spotlighted, men are pitted against each other in one-on-one mirror-like combat in order to release energies in themselves and in their audience that are demonic by the standards of ordinary—or do I mean noncombative?—life. The triumphant boxer is Satan transmogrified as Christ, as one senses sitting amid a delirium-swept crowd like the one that cheered Mike Tyson on to victory. Yet, even before Tyson began to fight, even before he entered the ring, the crowd was fixed upon him emotionally. (As the crowd was fixed, more evenly, upon Marvin Hagler and Thomas Hearns in their April 1985 match, shrieking as soon as the men appeared and scarcely stopping until the fight itself was stopped after eight very long minutes. Ecstasy precedes stimulus and may, indeed, help bring it into being.) For many, Mike Tyson has become the latest in a lineage of athletic heroes—a bearer of inchoate, indescribable emotion—a savior, of sorts, covered in sweat and ready for war. But then most saviors, sacred or secular, are qualified by a thoughtful "of sorts." In any case, it's Tyson's turn. A terrible beauty is born.

Other than boxing, everything is so boring.
— MIKE TYSON

Las Vegas, Nevada. March 7, 1987. In a ring still stained with blood from the desperately fought heavyweight match that preceded it, Mike Tyson, World Boxing Council champion, at twenty the youngest heavyweight titleholder in boxing history, brings the fight for unification of the title to James "Bonecrusher" Smith, World Boxing Association champion, at thirty-three an aging athlete, and, yet more telling, the only heavyweight titleholder in boxing history to have graduated from college—but Smith will have none of it. He clinches, he backs away, he walks away, he clinches again, hugging his frustrated and increasingly infuriated opponent like a drowning man hugging something—anything—that floats. Referee Mills Lane calls "Break!" repeatedly during the twelve long rounds of this very long fight but Smith seems not to hear; or, hearing, will not obey. For the most part his expression is blank, with the blankness of fear, a stark unmitigated fear without shame, yet shameful to witness. "Fight!" the crowd shouts. "Do something!" In the

ringside seats close by me Smith's fellow boxers Trevor
Berbick (former WBC heavyweight champion) and Edwin
Rosario (WBA lightweight champion) are particularly vo-
cal, as if in an agony of professional discomfort. For it
seems that the superbly conditioned Smith, who had performed so dramatically only three months ago in Madison
Square Garden, knocking out Tim Witherspoon in the
first round of his WBA title defense, is now, suddenly,
not a boxer: though in that elevated and garishly spotlighted ring with another man, contracted for $1 million
to fight him, performing in front of a crowd of some
13,600 people in the Hilton's newly erected outdoor sta-
dium, and how many millions of television viewers, he
cannot or will not fight. His instinct is merely to survive
—to get through twelve rounds with no injuries more serious than a bleeding left eye and a bad swelling on the
right side of his face; and to go back, professionally disgraced, to his wife, family, and plans for the future ("Being a champion opens lots of doors—I'd like to get a real
estate license, maybe sell insurance") in Magnolia, North
Carolina.

Berbick writhes in the folding chair beside me, mut-
tering, laughing, derisive, very nearly as frustrated as
Mike Tyson, and clearly resentful—after all, he is the
man who fought Tyson here last November, and so spectacularly (and humiliatingly) lost to him, in the third minute of the second round of that fight. He too had tried to
clinch with Tyson, had gripped the young man's arms and
gloves in an effort to hold him back, slow him down, frus-

trate him, but Berbick had also fought him, or made a game attempt—"I wanted to prove my manhood," he said afterward, ruefully, "that was my mistake." In this match Smith's manhood is not evidently an issue. He has no "machismo" to display or defend; if he is a boxer it must be by default. Minute follows minute, round follows grinding round, as Tyson tries to get inside to throw the rapid-fire combinations for which he is famous, and Smith falls upon him and hugs him, clumsily, defiantly, desperately. Mills Lane, exasperated, penalizes Smith by deducting points from him after rounds two and eight. ("I could have deducted a point from him after each round," he said afterward, "but you don't like to do that in a title fight.") The 6-foot-4-inch 233-pound Smith is a zombie tonight, a parody of a boxer, so resistant to boxing's visible and invisible rules, that complex of mores that make boxing at once the most primitive and the most sophisticated of contact sports, it is fascinating to watch him—to a degree.

"I wasn't prepared for how strong Tyson is, how fast," Smith will say after the fight. "Tyson has a devastating left hook." And, defensively: "I did the best I could." Of current heavyweights Smith has invariably been the most erratic in performance, the most unpredictable—capable, under pressure, of boxing well, yet strangely and unprofessionally susceptible to vagaries of mood. Perhaps because he has no real vocation as a boxer—and no more instinct for fighting than one might expect from a man with a B.A. in business administration (from Shaw College, North Carolina)—he is easily demoralized in the ring, allowing childlike expressions of triumph, hurt, bewilderment, and acute unhappiness to show on his face, as boxers so rarely do; he boxes as an intelligent man might box whose intelligence is his only weapon in an action in which "intelligence" must be subordinated to something more fundamental. He draws upon no deeper reserves of self—no energy, imagination, emotion—beyond those of consciousness.

As for Tyson: unlike Dempsey, Marciano, and Frazier, those famously aggressive fighters to whom he is often compared, Tyson is not a reckless boxer; he is not willing, as so many boxer-fighters are, to take four or five punches in order to throw a punch of his own. His training is defensive and cautious—hence the peek-a-boo stance, a Cus D'Amato signature: for is not boxing primarily the art of self-defense? of hitting your man, and scoring points, without being hit in return? For two years, which must have been very long years, D'Amato trained Tyson to bob, weave, slip punches from sparring partners without throwing a single punch in response—a conditioning that has made Tyson an anomaly in the ring. His reputation is for power, speed, and aggression, but his defensive skills are as remarkable, if less dramatic. Confronted with an opponent like "Bonecrusher" Smith, who violates the decorum of the ring by not fighting, Tyson is at a loss; he hits his man after the bell, in an adolescent display of frustration; he exchanges insults with him during the fight, makes jeering faces; pushes, shoves, laces the cut over Smith's eye during a clinch; betrays those remnants of his Brooklyn street-fighting days (Tyson, as a child of ten, was one of the youngest members of a notorious gang called the Jolly Stompers) his training as a boxer should have overcome. In short, his inexperience shows.

So the pattern of the fight is immediately established: in the entire twelve rounds virtually nothing will happen that does not happen in the first thirty seconds of the first round. The spectator is gripped by stasis itself, by the perversity of the expectation that, against all expectation, something will happen. If this is theater, and boxing is always theater, we are in the slyly teasing anti-worlds of Jarry, Ionesco, Beckett; the aesthetics is that of fanatic tedium, as in John Cage and Andy Warhol. While my press colleagues to a man will report the match boring —"Two interior decorators could have done each other more damage" *(Los Angeles Times)*—I find it uniquely tense, and exhausting; not unlike the first Spinks/Holmes fight in which the frustrated Holmes carried his right glove for round after round, a talismanic club waiting to be swung. Poor Holmes! Poor Lear! This is the very poetry of masculine frustration—the failure of psychic closure. Such fights end, and are funny, in retrospect; but are never resolved.

Tyson's predicament vis-à-vis "Bonecrusher" Smith brings to mind Jack Dempsey, similarly frustrated in his matches with Tunney, shouting at his retreating opponent, "Come on and fight!" But, for all his renown, Dempsey was not a strategic boxer of the sort Tyson has been meticulously trained to be; his ring style was virtually nonstop offense with very little defense, which means that he was willing to take punches in the hope of throwing his own. Outboxed by the more cautious and more intelligent Tunney, he eventually lost both fights. In the Tyson/Smith match there is no question that Tyson is the superior boxer; he will win every round unanimously in what is in fact one of the easiest fights of his two-year career as a professional. But this is hardly the dramatic public performance he'd hoped to give, and the fight's promoters had hoped to present. No knockout—none of the dazzling combinations of blows for which he is known; very little of what D'Amato taught his protégés was the boxer's primary responsibility to his audience: to entertain. Winning too can be a kind of failure.

The fight recalls several previous fights of Tyson's with opponents who, out of fear or cunning, or both, refused to fight him; yet more worrisomely it recalls Joe Louis's predicament as heavyweight champion in those years when, after having cleared the heavyweight division of all serious contenders, he was reduced to fighting mere opponents—"Bums-of-the-Month" as the press derisively called them. Worse, Louis's reputation as a puncher, a machine for hitting, so intimidated opponents that they were frightened to enter the ring with him. ("Enter the ring? My man had to be helped down the aisle," one manager is said to have said.) For a sport routinely attacked for its brutality boxing has had its share of historically

shameful episodes: Louis's title defense against a long-
forgotten challenger named Pastor, whom he chased for
ten dreary rounds of running and clutching, running and
clutching, is invariably cited. While Rocky Marciano/
Jersey Joe Walcott I (September 1952) was notable for
both fighters' courage—this was the fight that gave Marciano the heavyweight title—the rematch eight months
later ended with the first punch thrown by Marciano:
Walcott sat on the canvas and made no effort to get up as
he was counted out. ("After twenty-three years as a professional fighter, the former champion went out in a total
disgrace that no excuses can relieve"—Red Smith, a former admirer of Walcott.) Both Muhammad Ali/Sonny
Liston title matches were memorable for Liston's surpris-
ing behavior: in the first, in which Liston was defending
his title, he refused to continue fighting after the sixth
round, claiming a shoulder injury; in the second, he went
down with mysterious alacrity at one minute forty-eight
seconds of the first round, struck by a devastating, if invisible, blow to the head. (This defeat disgraced Liston
and effectively ended his career: he was never to be
offered another championship fight. Even the circumstances of his death some years later at the age of thirty-
eight were suspicious.) There was Dempsey's notorious
fight with Tommy Gibbons in Shelby, Montana, in 1923,
which made money for Dempsey and his promoter,
Kearns, while nearly bankrupting the town; there was the
bizarre "Slapsie" Maxey Rosenbloom, world light-
heavyweight champion of the early 1930s, a sort of paci-

fist of boxing, whose strategy was to hit (or slap, gloves open) and run—a boxing style as exciting to watch, it is said, as the growth of tree rings. While no one has ever questioned Marvelous Marvin Hagler's integrity, his defense of his middleweight title against Roberto Durán some years ago left many observers skeptical—the usually aggressive Hagler seemed oddly solicitous of his opponent. But the most scandalous boxing incident of modern times still remains Durán's decision, two minutes and forty-four seconds into the eighth round of his welterweight title defense with Sugar Ray Leonard in 1980, to simply quit the fight—"*No mas¡*" No more! Leonard had been outboxing him, making a fool of him, and Durán had had enough. Machismo punctures easily.

Though most of Mike Tyson's twenty-eight fights have ended with knockouts, often in early rounds, and once (with Joe Frazier's hapless son Marvis) within thirty seconds of the first round, several opponents have slowed him down as "Bonecrusher" Smith has done, and made him appear baffled, thwarted, intermittently clumsy. "Quick" Tillis and Mitch Green come most readily to mind; and, though Tyson eventually knocked him out, in the final round of a ten-round fight, José Ribalta. Perhaps the ugliest fight of Tyson's career was with Jesse Ferguson, who, in a performance anticipating Smith's, held onto him with such desperation after Tyson had broken his nose that even the referee could not free the men. (Ferguson was disqualified and the fight was ruled a TKO for Tyson.) Such performances do not constitute boxing at its finest moments, nor do they presage well for Tyson's future: to be a great champion one must have great opponents.

Incongruity, like vulgarity, is not a concept in Las Vegas. This fantasyland for adults, with its winking neon skyline, its twenty-four-hour clockless casinos, its slots, craps, Keno, roulette, baccarat, blackjack et al., created by fiat when the Nevada legislature passed a law legalizing gambling in 1931, exists as a counterworld to our own. There is no day here—the enormous casinos are pure interiority, like the inside of a skull. Gambling, as François Mauriac once said, is continuous suicide: if suicide, yet continuous. There is no past, no significant future, only an eternal and always optimistic present tense. Vegas is our exemplary American city, a congeries of hotels in the desert, shrines of chance in which, presumably, we are all equal as we are not equal before the law, or God, or one another. One sees in the casinos, especially at the slot machines, those acres and acres of slot machines, men and women of all ages, races, types, degrees of probable or improbable intelligence, as hopefully attentive to their machines as writers and academicians are to their word processors. If one keeps on, faithfully, obsessively, one will surely hit The Jackpot. (You know it's The Jackpot when your machine lights up, a goofy melody ensues, and a flood of coins like a lascivious Greek god comes tumbling into your lap.) The reedy dialects of irony—the habitual tone of the cultural critic in twentieth-century America—are as foreign here as snow, or naturally green grass.

So it is hardly incongruous that boxing matches are held in the Las Vegas Hilton and Caesar's Palace, VIP tickets at $1,000 or more (and the cheapest tickets, at $75, so remote from the ring that attendance at a fight is merely nominal, or symbolic); it is not incongruous that this most physical of sports, like the flipping of cards or the throw of dice, is more brilliantly realized as a gambling opportunity. In the elaborately equipped sports rooms of the big casinos, where television screens monitor various sporting events, sans sound, and betting statistics are constantly being posted, like stock market reports, one can bet on virtually any sport provided it is "professional" and not "amateur." The favorites are naturally baseball, football, basketball, boxing, and, of course, horseracing, the sport that seems to have been invented purely for gambling purposes. In these semidarkened rooms gamblers sit entranced, or comatose, drinks in hand, staring up at the television monitors and the hundreds, or is it thousands, of postings. Red numerals against a black background. A dozen or more television screens in an electronic collage. The upcoming "fight of the century"—Marvelous Marvin Hagler/Sugar Ray Leonard for Hagler's undisputed middleweight title, 6 April 1987 at Caesar's Palace—is the casinos' dream: as of 7 March odds are posted −3.25 Hagler, +2.25 Leonard, with these propositions: (1) the fight does not go twelve rounds; (2) Hagler by KO; (3) Hagler by decision; (4)

Leonard by KO; (5) Leonard by decision. The Mike Tyson /"Bonecrusher" Smith odds are Tyson −7.00, Smith +5.00, which means that you would make a good deal of money betting on Smith, if Smith would only win. Since Tyson's victory is a foregone conclusion the bookmakers offer only one proposition: that the fight does, or does not, go four rounds. (Which accounts for the outburst of ec static cheering, the only cheering of the fight, when the bell rings sounding the end of round four and Smith, bleeding down the left side of his face, freshly admonished by Mills Lane for holding and refusing to break, nonetheless walks to his corner.)

While in the antebellum American South white slaveowners frequently pitted their Negro slaves against each other in fights of spectacular savagery, and made bets on the results, in Las Vegas the descendants of these slaves, and their black kinsmen from the West Indies, Africa, and elsewhere, freely fight one another for purses of gratifying generosity: the highest paid athletes in the world are American boxers, and the highest paying fights are always in Vegas. Marvin Hagler, for instance, earned a minimum of $7.5 million for his April 1985 title defense against Thomas Hearns, who earned $7 million; in April 1987 he is guaranteed a minimum of $11 million against Leonard's $10 million in a fight that boxing promoters anticipate will make more money than any boxing match in history. ("I'm sure there will be $100,000 bets on both fighters," says a casino proprietor, "and we'll be right here to take them.") Mike Tyson will earn a minimum of $1.5 million for his fight with Smith (to Smith's $1 million) and if his spectacular career continues as everyone predicts, he will soon be earning as much as Hagler and Leonard, if not more. Though Tyson lacks Muhammad Ali's inspired narcissism, he is not handicapped by Ali's brash black politics and Ali's penchant for antagonizing whites: for all his reserve, his odd, even eerie combination of shyness and aggression, his is a wonderfully *marketable* image. (See the iconic "Mike Tyson" of billboard and newspaper ads, a metallic man, no twenty-year-old but a robot of planes, angles, inhuman composure: "Iron Mike" Tyson.)

Yet how subdued the real Tyson appeared, following the inglorious fight, and the noisy press conference in a candy-striped tent in a corner of the Hilton's parking lot: one caught glimpses of him that night at the jammed victory party on the thirtieth floor of the hotel, being interviewed, photographed, televised, and, later, being led through the hotel's crowded lobby, surrounded by publicity people, still being televised, wearing his preposterously ornate WBC champion's belt around his waist and his newly acquired WBA belt slung over his shoulder, his expression vague, dim, hooded, very possibly embarrassed ("It was a long, boring fight—twelve rounds"), like one of those captive demigods or doomed kings recorded in Frazer's *Golden Bough*.

What is "taboo" except that aspect of us that lies undefined, and inaccessible to consciousness: the core of impersonality within the carefully nurtured and jealously prized "personality" with which we are identified, by ourselves and others. In his speculative essay *Totem and Taboo* Freud meditated upon the ambivalent nature of taboo: its association with the sacred and consecrated, and with the dangerous, uncanny, forbidden, and unclean. All that one can say with certitude about taboo is that it stands in perennial opposition to the ordinary—to the quotidian. Taboo has to do with the numinous, with the ineffable, with utter indefinable mystery: with something not us. Or so we tell ourselves.

To the boxing aficionado the sport's powerful appeal is rarely exponible. It seems to be rooted in its paradoxical nature—the savagery that so clearly underlies, yet is contained by, its myriad rules, regulations, traditions, and superstitions. It seems to make the quotidian that which is uncanny, dangerous, forbidden, and unclean: it ritualizes violence, primarily male violence, to the degree to which violence becomes an aesthetic principle. In this, men's bodies (or, rather, their highly trained employment of their bodies) are instruments and not mere flesh like our own. That a man as a boxer is an action, and no longer a man, or not significantly a "man," puzzles those of us who feel ourselves fully defined in any of our actions. The romantic principles of Existentialism in its broadest, most vernacular sense have much to do with one's volition and one's will in creating oneself as an ethical being by way of a freely chosen action. Boxing, more than most contemporary American sports, clearly inhabits a dimension of human behavior one might call meta-ethical or meta-existential. There is no evident relationship between the man outside the ring and the man inside the ring—the boxer who is, like Mike Tyson (or Joe Louis, or Rocky Marciano, or any number of other boxers of distinction), "courteous," "soft-spoken," "gentle," in private life, and, in the ring, once the bell has sounded, "brutal," "awesome," "murderous," "devastating," "a young bull"—and the rest. The aim is not to kill one's opponent, for one's opponent is after all one's brother: the aim is to render him temporarily incapacitated, in a simulation of death. "It's unbelievable," Mike Tyson has said of boxing. "It's like a drug; I thrive on it. It's the excitement of the event, and now I need that excitement all the time."

When the boxer enters the ring, ceremonially disrobes, and answers the summons to fight, he ceases being an individual with all that implies of a socially regulated ethical bond with other individuals; he becomes a boxer, which is to say an action. It might be argued that America's fascination with sports—if "fascination" is not too weak a word for such frenzied devotion, weekend after weekend, season after season, in the lives of a majority of men—has to do not only with the power of taboo to violate, or transcend, or render obsolete conventional categories of morality, but with the dark, denied, muted, eclipsed, and wholly unarticulated underside of America's religion of success. Sports is only partly about winning; it is also about losing. Failure, hurt, ignominy, disgrace, physical injury, sometimes even death—these are facts of life, perhaps the very bedrock of lives, which the sports-actor, or athlete, must dramatize in the flesh; and always against his will. Boxing as dream-image, or nightmare, pits self against self, identical twin against twin, as in the womb itself where "dominancy," that most mysterious of human hungers, is first expressed. Its most characteristic moments of ecstasy—the approach to the knockout, the knockout, the aftermath of the knockout, and, by way of television replays, the entire episode retraced in slow motion *as in the privacy of a dream—* are indistinguishable from obscenity, horror. In the words of middleweight Sugar Ray Seales, 1972 Olympic Gold Medalist, a veteran of more than four hundred amateur and professional fights who went blind as a consequence of ring injuries: "I went into the wilderness, and fought the animals there, and when I came back I was blind."

In Clifford Geertz's classic anthropological essay of 1972, "Deep Play: Notes on the Balinese Cockfight," the point is made that, in Bali, the now-illegal cockfighting obsession is wholly male, and masculine: the "cock" is the male organ, as the Balinese freely acknowledge, but it is more than merely that—it is the man, the maleness, codified, individualized, in a context of other individuals: which is to say, society. The cockfight is utterly mind-less, bloody, savage, *animal*—and ephemeral: though a Balinese loves his fighting cock, and treats him tenderly, once the cock is dead it is dead, and quickly forgotten. (Sometimes, in a paroxysm of disappointment and rage,

Geertz notes, cock-owners dismember their own cocks after the cocks are killed.) Boxing in the United States is
far more complex a cultural phenomenon than the Balinese cockfight—it has much to do, for example, with im-
migrant succession, and with the ever-shifting tensions of
race—but some of the principles Geertz isolates in the
cockfight are surely operant: men are fascinated by boxing because it suggests that masculinity is measured
solely in terms of other men, and not in terms of women;
and because, in its very real dangers, it is a species of
"deep play" (an action in which stakes are so high that it
is, from a utilitarian standpoint, irrational for men to en-
gage in it at all) that seems to demonstrate the way the
world really is and not the way it is said, or wished, or
promised to be. The boxer is consumed in action, and has
no significant identity beyond action; the fight is a con-
vulsion of a kind, strictly delimited in space (a meticulously squared circle bounded, like an animal pen, by
ropes) and time. (Jack Dempsey, in whose honor the term
"killer instinct" was coined, once remarked that he wasn't
the fighter he might have been, with so many rules and
regulations governing the sport: "You're in there for
three-minute rounds with gloves on and a referee. That's
not real fighting.") The passions it arouses are always in
excess of its "utilitarian" worth since in fact it has none.
As the bloody, repetitious, and ephemeral cockfight is a
Balinese reading of Balinese experience, a story Balinese
men tell themselves about themselves, so too is the American boxing match a reading of American experience, un-

sentimentalized and graphic. Yes, one thinks, you have told us about civilized values; you have schooled us in the virtues, presumably Christian, of turning the other cheek; of meekness as a prerequisite for inheriting the earth— the stratagems (manipulative? *feminine?*) of indirection. But the boxing match suggests otherwise, and it is that reading of life that we prefer. The boxers make visible what is invisible in us, thereby defining us, and themselves, in a single consecrated action. As Rocky Graziano once said, "The fight for survival is the fight."

It's like being in love with a woman. She can be unfaithful, she can be mean, she can be cruel, but it doesn't matter. If you love her, you want her, even though she can do you all kinds of harm. It's the same with me and boxing. It can do me all kinds of harm, but I love it.
—*FLOYD PATTERSON,*
former heavyweight champion of the world

I t is the boxing match with the distinct premise as its theoretical axis that is likely to be the most profound, and in our time the boxer whose matches are most consistently fueled by such interior—if rarely articulated—logic is Mike Tyson, the youngest undisputed world heavyweight champion in history.

The premise underlying Tyson's first title match, for instance, with World Boxing Council titleholder Trevor Berbick, which Tyson won in six brilliantly executed minutes, was that a boxer of such extreme youth (Tyson was twenty at the time, and fighting in a division in which boxers customarily mature late), who had never fought any opponent approaching Berbick's quality, could nonetheless impose his will upon the older boxer: thus Tyson was a "challenger" in more than the usual sense of the word, as, for instance, the luckless Marvis Frazier, son of Joe, had been in challenging Larry Holmes for his heavyweight title some years before.

The premise underlying Tyson's second title defense in Atlantic City, on 16 October 1987, was something along these lines: the twenty-six-year-old challenger, Tyrell Biggs, an Olympic Gold Medalist in the superheavyweight division in 1984, deserved to be punished for having enjoyed a smoother and more triumphant career as an amateur than Mike Tyson; and deserved to be punished particularly badly because, in Tyson's words, "He didn't show me any respect." (Tyson said, post-fight, that he could have knocked out Biggs in the third round but chose to knock him out slowly "so that he would remember it for a long time. I wanted to hurt him real bad.") That emotions between the boxers' managers ran high before the match, very nearly to the point of hysteria, did not assuage the situation.

As with the young, pre-champion Dempsey, there is an unsettling air about Tyson, with his impassive death's-head face, his unwavering stare, and his refusal to glamorize himself in the ring—no robe, no socks, only the signature black trunks and shoes—that the violence he unleashes against his opponents is somehow just; that some hurt, some wound, some insult in his past, personal or ancestral, will be redressed in the ring; some mysterious imbalance righted. The single-mindedness of his ring style works to suggest that his grievance has the force of a natural catastrophe. That old trope, "the wrath of God," comes to mind.

Though there were boxing experts who persisted in thinking that Tyrell Biggs, with his "superior" boxing skills, and his height and reach advantage, could manage an upset against Tyson, for most spectators in the Atlantic City Convention Center the fight was a foregone conclusion. (The odds were ten to one in Tyson's favor.) Not which boxer would win but when would Tyson win, and how decisively, was the issue; and how badly after all would Biggs be hurt. Thus, when Biggs entered the ring, dancing, bobbing and weaving, shadow boxing, a singularly graceful figure in a white satin robe to mid-thigh, with built-up shoulders and fancy trim, accompanied by a sinister sort of music with a jungle-sounding beat, amplified but muffled, the vision was both alarming and eerily beautiful: for here was, not the champion's opponent, but the evening's sacrifice to the champion.

It is difficult to suggest to those whose experience of boxing has been limited to television how very different, and dramatically different, the "live" event is. For one thing, the live match is not filtered through the scrim of announcers' voices; it is voiceless, unmediated. Since words do not encompass it or define it one is not distracted by concepts, nor is one likely to know, from second to second, precisely what is happening, because it happens so swiftly, and irrevocably: no slow-motion replays. Announcers, too, develop homey, formulaic ways of talking about boxing; domesticating it, in a sense—as mellow-voiced narrators of African veldt documentaries domesticate the savage "natural" events of the animated food cycle. By naming, by conceptualizing, we reduce the horror of certain intransigent facts of life; by making the unspeakable speakable we bring it into a comfortable apotropaic relationship with us. Or delude ourselves that we have done so.

The live boxing match, however, suggests that such strategies are of no avail, and the more ferocious the fight, the more relentless the stalking of one man by the other, the wearing-down, the out-psyching, the approach to the knockout and the knockout itself, the more spell-binding the event. If refusing to look at the gouging out of Gloucester's eyes in *King Lear* could prevent that action, there would be some logic in refusing to look, but the event does occur, must occur, and by the terms of the contract we must watch. It is our obligation to the victim to witness, not his defeat, but the integrity with which he bears his defeat.

Real courage is required when you lose, Floyd Patterson once said. Winning is easy.

Matches of such spectacular action as Tyson/Berbick and Tyson/Biggs (arguably Tyson's most intelligently fought fight thus far) suggest boxing's kinship with ancient, or not-so-ancient, rites of sacrifice. The trappings of sport, let alone entertainment, simply dissolve away. One is witnessing the oldest story of our species, the battering of one man into submission by another, the triumph

of one which is the loss (the mock death) of the other; but
the significant issue, in boxing at least, is not this battering so much as the victim's accommodation of it, second
after second, round after terrible round.

Like his predecessor Pinklon Thomas, whom Tyson
handily knocked out to retain his World Boxing Association title, Tyrell Biggs was remarkably courageous in
absorbing Tyson's hammerlike blows, those left hooks in
particular, so that the theme of the fight as a drama became Biggs's quixotic, doomed determination in the face
of Tyson's single-minded assault. The fascination lay in
how long Biggs could endure it, or how long his cornermen would allow him to endure it. (What a surprise to afterward see the fight as Home Box Office televised it, and
to hear Sugar Ray Leonard wonder aloud repeatedly why
Biggs had "abandoned" his game plan—as if the helpless
boxer had had any choice in the matter.) Biggs's strategy
of lateral movement, quick jabs, constant motion was
thwarted almost immediately, confronted by Tyson's superior will and strength; his much-publicized jab was
a flicking sort of jab, a stay-away-from-me jab, while
Tyson's newly honed jab was the real thing, a blow (with
which, in the second round, Tyson split open Biggs's lip).
In retrospect the match seemed a mis-match, like so
many of Tyson's thirty-odd matches, but only in retrospect, since at the start—at the very start, at least—Biggs
seemed to have had a chance. It was Tyson's unremitting
pressure, the intensity of his concentration, his will to do
hurt, that must have broken Biggs's spirit even before

his blows began to take their toll, for never in Tyson's career had he seemed so grimly resolute, so fixed upon destruction, and so exhausting to watch. The tiredness that must have seeped into the marrow of Biggs's bones, not to drain away, perhaps, for months, or years, was felt throughout the arena, a counterpoint to the nerved-up exhilaration of Tyson's attack. (Surely he is the oldest twenty-one-year-old on record?) Tyson has said that he doesn't think in the ring but acts intuitively; like his great predecessor Joe Louis, but unlike, for instance, Muhammad Ali, he gives the chilling impression of being a machine for hitting, and in this most rococo of his fights a machine for rapid and repeated extra-legal maneuvers— low blows, using his elbows, hitting after the bell. Never has a fight, in my limited experience at least, been so oppressively *communal* . . . as if we were all trapped inside the ring's foursquare geometry, with no way out except to be knocked through the ropes, as Biggs would be, at last, in the seventh round. And no way to be saved from annihilation except to succumb to it.

The tension generated by a typical Tyson fight— meaning one controlled and dominated by him—must be experienced to be understood. Tyson/Biggs struck its tone of high expectancy even before Tyson entered the arena (robeless, but wearing the three oversized and absurdly ornamental belts that are the warrior-symbols of his three titles) and built steadily, in some quarters very nearly unbearably, to its climax in the seventh round, when the blood-bespattered referee, Tony

Orlando, stopped the fight after the second knockdown without counting over Biggs. Tyson's ring style, pitiless, forward-moving, seemingly invincible, evokes odd behavior in presumably normal people. Do most men identify with Tyson-as-potential-killer? Do most women identify with Tyson's victims? Or is "identification" in terms of the fight, the spectacle, the playing-out-of-action itself? When a great fight occurs—and Tyson has not yet had a great fight, for the reason that he has not yet had a worthy opponent—the spectator experiences something like the mysterious catharsis of which Aristotle wrote, the purging of pity and terror by the exercise of these emotions; the subliminal aftermath of classical tragedy.

These fights do linger in the mind, sometimes obsessively, like nightmare images one can't quite expel, but the actual experience of the fight, in the arena, is a confused, jolting, and sometimes semihysterical one. The reason is primary, or you might say primitive: either Tyson is hitting his man, or he is preparing to hit his man, and if nothing nasty happens within the next few seconds it will not be for Tyson's not trying. (For a man of Tyson's physical build he is extraordinarily fast with his hands, and he hits in combinations.) In the average boxing match, contrary to critics' charges of "barbarism," "brutality," et al., nothing much happens, as boxing aficionados affably accept, but in Tyson fights (with one obvious exception—the 7 March 1987 title fight with "Bonecrusher" Smith) everything can happen, and sometimes does.

Thus individuals in the audience behave oddly, and involuntarily—there was even a scuffle or an actual fight at the rear of the Convention Hall during the third or fourth round of the fight in the ring, not suggested by the television coverage, and a matter of some confused alarm until security guards broke it up. Some women hid their faces, some men emitted not the stylized cries of "Hit him!" or even "Kill him!" but parrotlike shrieks that seemed to be torn from them—perhaps the "womanlike" shrieks Tyson amusingly described coming from Biggs when he was hit. The boxing commissioner for New York State, ex-world lightheavyweight champion José Torres, seemed to forget himself as he shouted out commands to Tyson (who was oblivious to him as to everyone and everything outside the ring) and to Tyson's cornermen (who were too far away to have heard, should they have wished to hear). Torres's violent hand signals and shouted commands—"Six-five!" was one—would have seemed quite mysterious, if not deranged, had one not known that Torres, like Tyson, is a former D'Amato protégé, and had one not guessed that the ex-champion simply could not resist participating in the mesmerizing action. Strangest of all—and discreetly ignored by HBO television cameras—a fight threatened to ensue between Biggs's chief cornerman, the redoubtable Lou Duva, and the fight's promoter, Don King himself, at the immediate conclusion of the match; each man had to be forcibly restrained from rushing at the other. While television audiences watched the triumphant Tyson striding about the ring, and the dazed Biggs sitting on the canvas, attended by a physician, most of us were watching fascinated as the portly, not-young Lou Duva tried to climb through the ropes to get at Don King at ringside, the two gentlemen shouting at each other, for reasons only a few insiders would know: King had wanted the fight stopped immediately after the first knockdown, fearing "slaughter," but Duva had insisted that the fight continue, no matter the risk to Biggs. Duva had his way, and the fight continued a few more seconds, as if to fulfill its premise—Biggs deserved to be hurt, and to be hurt "real bad" by Tyson.

Boxing's spectacle is degrading, no doubt—in the most primary sense of the word: a de-grading of the self; a breaking-down, as if one's sensitive nerve-endings were being worn away. That the losing, failing, staggering boxer will not quit is very much a part of the degradation process, for boxing is as much about losing as winning, about being hurt as doing hurt, and even the most macho of spectators is roused to sympathy with the boxer who, though losing, has displayed that "grace" and "courage" of which, in another context, Hemingway spoke.

When the fight was over people remained for some minutes in their seats as if spellbound or dazed, like Biggs; or exhausted—the twenty minutes of action had seemed rather more like twenty hours. The prospect of surrendering Mike Tyson's display of *control* to the quotidian *controllessness* of the world seemed daunting, but we made our way, a crowd of thousands, milling and surging, headless, directionless—the yellow-clad ushers, so much in evidence earlier, seemed now to have entirely vanished—through dour dirty passageways with no EXIT signs and into cul-de-sacs of some terror, for what if, we were all thinking, what if there is a fire? a sudden panic? and we stampede one another to death? a fate some might consider only just, since we had all been witnesses to an action of indefensible savagery?—but, by sheer blind groping instinct, a sort of Brownian movement of human molecules, we made our way out to the street, or into underground passageways that led to the swanked-up tackiness of the Trump Plaza, where figured carpets in primary colors jolted the optic nerve and functionless silly mirrored columns blocked pedestrian movement, showing us what we could not have wanted much to see, our own faces. The fight being over, the "real" world floods back, and the powerful appeal of Mike Tyson, as of his great predecessors, is that, in however artificial and delimited a context, a human being, *one of us*, reduced to the essence of physical strength, skill, and ingenuity, has control of his fate—if this control can manifest itself merely in the battering of another human being into absolute submission. This is not all that boxing is, but it is boxing's secret premise: life is hard in the ring, but, there, you only get what you deserve.

THE CRUELEST
SPORT

And if the body does not do fully
as much as the soul?
And if the body were not
the soul, what is the soul?
—*WALT WHITMAN,*
"I Sing the Body Electric"

A boxer's victory is gained in blood.
—*GREEK INSCRIPTION*

P rofessional boxing is the only major American sport whose primary, and often murderous, energies are not coyly deflected by such artifacts as balls and pucks. Though highly ritualized, and as rigidly bound by rules, traditions, and taboos as any religious ceremony, it survives as the most primitive and terrifying of contests: two men, near-naked, fight each other in a brightly lit, elevated space roped in like an animal pen (though the ropes were originally to keep rowdy spectators out); two men climb into the ring from which only one, symbolically, will climb out. (Draws do occur in boxing, but are rare, and unpopular.) Boxing is a stylized mimicry of a fight to the death, yet its mimesis is an uncertain convention, for boxers do sometimes die in the ring, or as a consequence of a bout; their lives are sometimes, perhaps always, shortened by the stress and punishment of their careers (in training camps no less than in official fights). Certainly, as in the melancholy case of Muhammad Ali, the most acclaimed and beloved heavyweight in boxing history, the quality of the boxer's post-retirement life is frequently diminished. For the great majority of boxers, past and present, life in the ring is nasty, brutish, and short—and not even that remunerative.

Yet, for inhabitants of the boxing world, the ideal conclusion of a fight is a knockout, and not a decision; and this, ideally, not the kind in which a man is counted "out" on his feet, still less a TKO ("technical knockout"—from injuries), but a knockout in the least ambiguous sense—one man collapsed and unconscious, the other leaping about the ring with his gloves raised in victory, the very embodiment of adolescent masculine fantasy. Like a tragedy in which no one dies, the fight lacking a classic knockout always seems unresolved, unfulfilled: the strength, courage, ingenuity, and desperation of neither boxer have been adequately measured. Catharsis is but partial, the Aristotelian principle of an action complete in itself has been thwarted. (Recall the fury of young Muhammad Ali at the too-readily-defeated Sonny Liston in their second, notorious title fight, of 1965: instead of going to a neutral corner, Ali stood over his fallen opponent with his fist cocked, screaming, "Get up and fight, sucker!") This is because boxing's mimesis is not that of a mere game, but a powerful analogue of human struggle in the rawest of life-and-death terms. When the analogue is not evoked, as, in most fights, it is not, the action is likely to be unengaging, or dull; "boxing" is an art, but "fighting" is the passion. The delirium of the crowd at one of those matches called "great" must be experienced first-hand to be believed (Frazier-Ali I, 1971, Hagler-Hearns, 1986, for instance); identification with the fighters is so intense, it is as if barriers between egos dissolve, and one is in the presence of a Dionysian rite of cruelty, sacrifice, and redemption. "The nearest thing to death," Ali described it, after his third title match with Joe Frazier, in 1975, which he won when the fight was stopped after the fourteenth round. Or: "This is some way to make a living, isn't it?" as the superlightweight Saoul Mamby said, badly battered after a title fight with the champion Billy Costello, in 1984.

A romance of (expendable) maleness—in which The Fight is honored, and even great champions come, and go.

For these reasons, among others, boxing has long been America's most popularly despised sport: a "so-called" sport, even a "meta-" or an "anti-" sport: a "vicious exploitation of maleness" as prostitution and pornography may be said to be a vicious exploitation of femaleness. It is not, contrary to common supposition, the most dangerous sport (the American Medical Association, arguing for boxing's abolition, acknowledges that it is statistically less dangerous than speedway racing, Thoroughbred racing, downhill skiing, professional football, et al.), but it is the most spectacularly and pointedly cruel sport, its intention being to stun one's opponent's brain; to affect the orgasmic communal "knockout" that is the culminating point of the rising action of the ideal fight. The humanitarian argues that boxing's very *intentionality* is obscene, which sets it apart, theoretically at least, from the purer (i.e., Caucasian) Establishment sports bracketed above. Boxing is only possible if there is an endless supply of young men hungry to leave their impoverished ghetto neighborhoods, more than willing to substitute the putative dangers of the ring for the more evident, possibly daily, dangers of the street; yet it is rarely advanced as a means of eradicating boxing, that poverty itself be abolished; that it is the social conditions feeding boxing that are obscene. The pious hypocrisy of Caucasian moralists vis-à-vis the sport that has become almost exclusively the province of black and ethnic minorities has its analogue in a classic statement of President Bush's, that he is worried by the amount of "filth" flooding America by way of televised hearings and trials: not that the Clarence Thomas-Anita Hill hearing and the William Kennedy Smith rape trial revealed "filth" at the core of certain male-female relations in our society, but that public airings of such, the very hearings and trials, are the problem. Ban the spectacle, and the obscenity will cease to exist.

The aesthetics of boxing is in sharp contrast to its ethics. Abjured by the referee, "Fight a good, clean fight, boys!" the boys need not ponder why a "good, clean fight" is, in fact, morally different from any other. Black boxers from the time of Jack Johnson (the first and most flamboyant of the world's black heavyweight champions, 1908–1915) through Joe Louis, Sugar Ray Robinson, Muhammad Ali, Larry Holmes, Sugar Ray Leonard and Mike Tyson have been acutely conscious of themselves as racially *other* from their audiences, whom they must please in one way or another, as black villains, or honorary whites. (After his pulverizing defeat of the "good, humble Negro" Floyd Patterson, in a heavyweight title match of 1962, Sonny Liston gloated in his role as black villain; when he lost so ingloriously to Muhammad Ali, a brash new-style black who drew upon Jack Johnson, Sugar Ray Robinson, and even the campy professional wrestler Gorgeous George for his own public persona, Liston lost his mistique, and his career soon ended.) To see race as a predominant factor in American boxing is inevitable, but the moral issues, as always in this paradoxical sport, are ambiguous. Is there a moral distinction between the spectacle of black slaves in the Old South being forced by their white owners to fight to the death, for purposes of gambling, and the spectacle of contemporary blacks fighting for multi-million-dollar paydays, for TV coverage from Las Vegas and Atlantic City? When, in 1980, in one of the most cynically promoted boxing matches in history, the aging and ailing Muhammad Ali fought the young heavyweight champion Larry Holmes, in an "execution" of a fight that was stopped after ten rounds, did it alleviate the pain, or the shame, that Ali was guaranteed $8 million for the fight? (Of which, with characteristic finesse, promoter Don King cheated him of nearly $1 million.) Ask the boxers.

Boxing today is very different from boxing of the past, which allowed a man to be struck repeatedly while trying to get to his feet (Dempsey-Willard, 1919), or to be knocked down seven times in three wholly one-sided rounds (Patterson-Johansson I, 1959), or so savagely and senselessly struck in the head with countless unanswered blows that he died in a coma ten days later (Griffith-Paret, 1962); the more immediate danger, for any boxer fighting a Don King opponent, is that the fight will be stopped prematurely, by a zealous referee protective of King's investment. As boxing is "reformed," it becomes less satisfying on a deep, unconscious level, more nearly resembling amateur boxing; yet, as boxing remains primitive, brutal, bloody, and dangerous, it seems ever more anachronistic, if not in fact obscene, in a society with pretensions of humanitarianism. Its exemplary figure is that of the warrior, of some mythopoetic time before weapons were invented; the triumph of physical genius, in a technologically advanced world in which the physical counts for very little, set beside intellectual skills. Even in the gritty world of the underclass, who, today, would choose to fight with mere *fists?* Guns abound, death to one's opponents at a safe distance is possible even for children. Mike Tyson's boast, after his defeat of the 12–1 underdog Carl Williams in a heavyweight title defense of 1989, "I want to fight, fight, fight and destruct the world," strikes a poignantly hollow note, even if we knew nothing of subsequent disastrous events in Tyson's life and career.

Consider the boxing trainer's time-honored adage: *They all go if you hit them right.*

These themes are implicit in Thomas Hauser's *Muhammad Ali: His Life and Times* and *The Black Lights: Inside the World of Professional Boxing;* but it is only in the latter work that theoretical, historical, and psychological issues are considered—Hauser sees boxing as "the red light district of professional sports" in which individuals of exceptional talent, courage, and integrity nonetheless prevail. His *Ali* is the heftier and more ambitious of the two, befitting its prodigious subject—the most famous athlete of all time, until recent years the most highly paid athlete of all time. An authorized biography, it would appear to be definitive, and is certainly exhaustive; Hauser spent thousands of hours with his subject, as well as approximately two hundred other people, and was given access to Ali's medical records. The text arranges these testimonies into a chronological history in which (is this New Age biography?) the author's voice alternates with, but rarely comments upon, still less criticizes, what these others have said. Compassionate, intelligent, fairminded, *Muhammad Ali: His Life and Times* might have benefited from further editing and paraphrase. Specific subjects (an imminent fight, financial deals, Ali's marital problems, Ali's health problems, the Nation of Islam, et al.) become lost in a welter of words; frequently, it is difficult to locate dates, even for important fights. And no ring record of Ali in the appendix!—a baffling omission, as if Ali's performance as an athlete were not the primary reason for this book.

As it happens, Hauser's succinct commentary on the Ali phenomenon and his shrewd analysis of the boxing world, including Don King's role in it, in *The Black Lights*, can provide, for the reader of the biography, a kind of companion gloss; the books are helpfully read in tandem. It is a remark of Ali's, in 1967, that gives *The Black Lights* its ominous title:

> *They say when you get hit and hurt bad you see black lights—the black lights of unconsciousness. But I don't know nothing about that. I've had twenty-eight fights and twenty-eight wins. I ain't never been stopped.*

Muhammad Ali, born Cassius Marcellus Clay in Louisville, Kentucky, on January 17, 1942, grandson of a slave, began boxing at the age of twelve, and, by eighteen, had fought one hundred and eight amateur bouts. How is it possible, the young man who, in his twenties, would astonish the world not just with the brilliance of his boxing but the sharpness of his wit, seemed to have been a dull-average student in high school who graduated 376th out of a class of 391; in 1966, his score on a mental aptitude test was an Army I.Q. of 78, well below military qualification. In 1975, Ali confessed to a reporter that he "can't read too good" and had not read ten pages of all the material written about him. I remember the television interview in which, asked what else he might have done with his life, Ali paused, for several seconds, clearly not knowing how to reply. All he'd ever known, he said finally, was boxing.

Mental aptitude tests cannot measure genius except in certain narrow ranges, and the genius of the body, the play of lightning-swift reflexes coupled with unwavering precision and confidence, eludes comprehension. All great boxers posses this genius, which scrupulous training hones, but can never create. "Styles make fights," as Ali's great trainer Angelo Dundee says, and "style" was young Ali's trademark. Yet even after early wins over such veterans as Archie Moore and Henry Cooper, the idiosyncracies of Ali's style aroused skepticism in boxing experts. After winning the Olympic gold medal in 1960, Ali was described by A.J. Leibling as "skittering... like a pebble over water." Everyone could see that this brash young boxer held his hands too low; he leaned away from punches instead of properly slipping them; his jab was light and flicking; he seemed to be perpetually on the brink of disaster. As a seven-to-one underdog in his first title fight with Sonny Liston, the twenty-two-year-old challenger astounded the experts with his performance, which was like none other they had ever seen in the heavyweight division; he so outboxed and demoralized Liston that Liston "quit on his stool" after the sixth round. A new era in boxing had begun, like a new music.

*"Ali rode the crest of a new wave of athletes—
competitors who were both big and fast . . . Ali had a
combination of size and speed that had never been
seen in a fighter before, along with incredible will
and courage. He also brought a new style to boxing.
Jack Dempsey changed fisticuffs from a kind where
fighters fought in a tense defensive style to a wild sen-
sual assault. Ali revolutionized boxing the way black
basketball players have changed basketball today. He
changed what happened in the ring, and elevated it
to a level that was previously unknown."*

(Larry Merchant, quoted in Hauser)

In the context of contemporary boxing—the sport is
in one of its periodic slumps—there is nothing more instructive and rejuvenating than to see again these old,
early fights of Ali's, when, as his happy boast had it, he
floated like a butterfly and stung like a bee and threw
punches faster than opponents could see—like the "mystery" right to the temple of Liston that felled him, in the
first minute of the first round of their rematch. These
early fights, the most brilliant being against Cleveland
Williams, in 1966, predate by a decade the long, grueling, punishing fights of Ali's later career whose cumula-
tive effects hurt Ali so irrevocably, resulting in what doc-
tors call, carefully, his "Parkinsonianism"—to distin-
guish it from "Parkinson's Disease." There is a true visceral shock in observing a heavyweight with the grace,
agility, swiftness of hands and feet, defensive skills and

ring cunning of a middleweight Ray Robinson, or a light-weight Willie Pep!—like all great athletes, Ali has to be seen to be believed. In a secular, yet pseudo-religious and sentimental nation like the United States, it is quite natural that sports stars emerge as "heroes"—"legends"—"icons." Who else? George Santayana described religion as "another world to live in" and no world is so *other*, so set off from the disorganization and disenchantment of the quotidian than the world, or worlds, of sports. Hauser describes, in considerable detail, the transformation of the birth of Ali out of the unexpectedly stubborn and idealistic will of young Cassius Clay: how, immediately following his first victory over Liston, he declared himself a convert to the Nation of Islam (more popularly known as the Black Muslims) and "no longer a Christian." He repudiated his "slave name" of Cassius Marcellus Clay to become Muhammad Ali. (A name which, incidentally, the *New York Times*, among other censorious white publications, would not honor through the 1960's.) Ali became, virtually overnight, a spokesman for black America as no other athlete, certainly not the purposefully reticent Joe Louis, had ever done—"I don't have to be what you want me to be," he told white, media-dominated America, "I'm free to be what I want to be." Two years later, refusing to be inducted into the army to fight in Vietnam, Ali, beleaguered by reporters, uttered one of the great, incendiary remarks of that era: "Man, I ain't got no quarrel with them Vietcong."

How ingloriously white America responded to Ali, how unashamedly racist and punitive: the government retaliated by overruling a judge who had granted Ali the status of conscientious objector, fined him $10,000 and sentenced him to five years in prison; outrageously, he was stripped of his heavyweight title and deprived of his license to box. Eventually, the U.S. Supreme Court would overturn the conviction, and, as the tide of opinion shifted in the country, in the early 1970's as the Vietnam War wound down, Ali returned triumphantly to boxing again, and regained the heavyweight title not once but twice. Years of exile during which he'd endured the angry self-righteousness of the conservative white press seemed, wonderfully, not to have embittered him. He had become a hero. He had entered myth.

Yet the elegiac title of Angelo Dundee's chapter in Dave Anderson's *In The Corner*—"We Never Saw Muhammad Ali at His Best"—defines the nature of Ali's sacrifice for his principles, and the loss to boxing. When, after the three-and-a-half-year layoff, Ali returned to the ring, he was of course no longer the seemingly invincible boxer he'd been; he'd lost his legs, thus his primary line of defense. Like the maturing writer who learns to replace the incandescent head-on energies of youth with what is called technique, Ali would have to descend into his physical being and experience for the first time the punishment ("the nearest thing to death") this is the lot of the great boxer willing to put himself to the test. As Ali's personal physician at that time, Ferdie Pacheco, said,

*[Ali] discovered something which was both very good
and very bad. Very bad in that it led to the physical
damage he suffered later in his career; very good in
that it eventually got him back the championship. He
discovered that he could take a punch.*

The secret of Ali's mature success, and the secret of his
tragedy: *he could take a punch.*

For the remainder of his twenty-year career, Muhammad Ali took punches, many of the kind that, delivered to
a non-boxer, would kill him or her outright—from Joe
Frazier in their three exhausting marathon bouts, from
George Foreman, from Ken Norton, Leon Spinks, Larry
Holmes. Where in his feckless youth Ali was a dazzling
figure combining, say, the brashness of Hotspur and the
insouciance of Lear's Fool, he became in these dark,
brooding, increasingly willed fights the closest analogue
boxing contains to Lear himself; or, rather, since there is
no great fight without two great boxers, the title matches
Ali-Frazier I (which Frazier won by a decision) and Ali-
Frazier III (which Ali won, just barely, when Frazier virtually collapsed after the fourteenth round) are boxing's
analogues to *King Lear*—ordeals of unfathomable human
courage and resilience raised to the level of classic tragedy. These somber and terrifying boxing matches make us
weep for their very futility; we seem to be in the presence
of human experience too profound to be named—beyond
the syntactical strategies and diminishments of language.

The mystic's dark night of the soul, transmogrified as a brutal meditation of the body.

And Ali-Foreman, Zaire, 1974: the occasion of the infamous "rope-a-dope" defense, by which the thirty-two-year-old Ali exhausted his twenty-six-year-old opponent by the inspired method of, simply, and horribly, allowing him to punch himself out on Ali's body and arms. This is a fight of such a magical quality that even to watch it closely is not to see how it was done, its fairy tale reversal in the eighth round executed. (One of Norman Mailer's most impassioned books, *The Fight*, is about this fight; watching a tape of Ali on the ropes enticing, and infuriating, and frustrating, and finally exhausting his opponent by an offense in the guise of a defense, I pondered what sly lessons of masochism Mailer absorbed from being at ringside that day, what deep-imprinted resolve to outwear all adversaries.)

These hard-won victories began irreversible loss: progressive deterioration of Ali's kidneys, hands, reflexes, stamina. By the time of that most depressing of modern-day matches, Ali-Holmes, 1980, when Ali was thirty-eight years old, Ferdie Pacheco had long departed the Ali camp, dismissed for having advised Ali to retire; those who supported Ali's decision to fight, like the bout's promoter Don King, had questionable motives. Judging from Hauser's information, it is a wonder that Ali survived this fight at all: the fight was, in Sylvester Stallone's words, "like watching an autopsy on a man who's still alive." (In *The Black Lights*, Hauser describes the bedlam that followed this vicious fight at Caesar's Palace, Las Vegas, where gamblers plunged in an orgy of gambling, as in a frenzy of feeding, or copulation: "Ali and Holmes had done their job.") Incredibly, Ali was allowed to fight once more, with Trevor Berbick, in December 1981, before retiring permanently.

Hauser's portrait of Ali is compassionate and unjudging: is the man to be blamed for having been addicted to his body's own adrenaline, or are others to be blamed for indulging him—and exploiting him? The brash rap-style egoism of young Cassius Clay underwent a considerable transformation during Ali's long public career, yet strikes us, perhaps, as altered only in tone: "Boxing was just to introduce me to the world," Ali has told his biographer. Mystically involved in the Nation of Islam, Ali sincerely believes himself an international emissary for peace, love, and understanding (he who once wreaked such violence upon his opponents!); and who is to presume to feel sorry for one who will not feel sorry for himself?

The Black Lights: Inside the World of Professional Boxing describes a small, self-contained arc—a few years in the career of a boxer named Billy Costello, at one time a superlightweight titleholder from Kingston, New York. Like *Muhammad Ali,* it is a sympathetic study of its primary subject, Costello, his manager Mike Jones, and their families and associates; yet, in the interstices of a compelling narrative taking us through the preparation for a successful title defense of 1984, it illuminates aspects of the boxing world generally unknown to outsiders—the routine and discipline of the boxer in training; the complex role of the fight manager; the exhausting contractual negotiations; the state of this "red-light district"—

> *"Professional boxing is no longer worthy of civilized society. It's run by self-serving crooks, who are called promoters . . .Except for the fighters, you're talking about human scum . . .Professional boxing is utterly immoral. It's not capable of reformation. I now favor the abolition of professional boxing. You'll never clean it up. Mud can never be clean."*
>
> (Howard Cosell, quoted in Hauser)

Like others sympathetic with boxers, who are in fact poorly paid, non-unionized workers with no benefits in a monopolistic business without antitrust control, Hauser argues strongly for a national association to regulate the sport; a federal advisory panel to protect boxers from exploitation. His portrait of Billy Costello allows us to see why a young man will so eagerly risk injuries in the ring, which is perceived as a life-line, and not a place of exploitation; why he will devote himself to the rigors of training in a sport in which, literally, one's entire career can end within a few seconds.

Black Lights ends dramatically, with Costello retaining his title against a thirty-seven-year-old opponent, Saoul Mamby, and with his hope of moving up in weight and making more money. Since its publication in 1986, the book has become a boxing classic; it is wonderfully readable, and, unlike *Ali*, judiciously proportioned. Yet to end the book with this victory is surely misleading, and even, to this reader, perplexing. The "black lights of unconsciousness" will be experienced by Billy Costello shortly, in a bout with a dazzlingly arrogant and idiosyncratic Ali-inspired young boxer named, at that time, "Lightning" Lonnie Smith, who would KO Costello in one of those nightmare scenarios all boxers have, before a hometown audience in Kingston. Following that devastating loss, Costello would fight the aging Alexis Arguello, one of the great lightweights of contemporary times, who would beat him savagely and end his career. To end with a tentative victory and not supply at least a coda to take us to the collapse of Billy Costello's career deprives *Black Lights* of the significance it might have had—for boxing is about failure far more than it is about success. In the words of the battered Saoul Mamby, "I'll miss it. I love boxing. Everything passed too soon."

ACKNOWLEDGMENTS

Anderson, Dave. *In The Corner: Great Boxing Trainers Talk About Their Art* (William Morrow, New York, 1991).

Anderson, Dave. Articles in *The New York Times*.

Berger, Phil. Articles in *The New York Times*.

Collins, Nigel. "Mike Tyson: The Legacy of Cus D'Amato," *The Ring*, February 1986.

Early, Gerald. *Tuxedo Junction: Essays on American Culture* (The Ecco Press, New Jersey, 1989).

Fried, Ronald K. *Corner Men: Great Boxing Trainers* (Four Walls, Eight Windows, New York, 1991).

Gorn, Elliot J. "The Manassa Mauler and the Fighting Marine: An Interpretation of the Dempsey-Tunney Fights," *Journal of American Studies*, Vol. 19 (1985).

Hauser, Thomas. *Muhammad Ali: His Life and Times* (Simon & Schuster, New York, 1991).

Hauser, Thomas. *The Black Lights: Inside the World of*

Professional Boxing (Simon & Schuster, New York, 1986, 1991).

Heller, Peter. *In This Corner: Forty World Champions Tell Their Stories* (Simon & Schuster, New York, 1973).

Illingworth, Montieth. *Mike Tyson: Money, Myth and Betrayal* (Birch Lane Press, New York, 1991).

McCallum, John D. *The World Heavyweight Boxing Championship: A History* (Chilton Book Co., Radnor, Pennsylvania, 1974).

McIlvanney, Hugh. *McIlvanney on Boxing: An Anthology* (Beaufort Books, New York, 1983).

Mead, Chris. *Champion: Joe Louis; Black Hero in White America* (Charles Scribner's Sons, New York, 1985).

Odd, Gilbert. *Encyclopedia of Boxing* (Crescent Books, New York, 1983).

The Ring magazine (New York, New York).

Schulian, John. *Writers' Fighters and Other Sweet Scientists* (Andrews & McMeel, Fairway, Kansas, 1983).

Background material for the section on "opponents" was drawn from articles by Michael Shapiro and Budd Schulberg appearing in *The New York Times* and *Newsday* respectively.

Sociologists David P. Phillips and John E. Hensley in "When Violence Is Rewarded or Punished: The Impact of Mass Media Stories on Homicide," *Journal of Communication*, Summer 1984, argue that highly publicized boxing matches have a direct and measurable effect upon the homicide rate, albeit with curious qualifications of race.

I am deeply indebted to my friend Ronald Levao of Rutgers University, who made available to me much of his collection of films and tapes of boxing matches from Johnson-Ketchel, 1909, to the present time, and whose advice and encouragement in the preparation of the manuscript has been invaluable.